Small Bites

Small Bites

Forty Short Stories

by

Don Tassone

Golden Antelope Press
715 E. McPherson
Kirksville, Missouri 63501
2018

ISBN: 978-1-936135-57-8 (1-936135-57-4)

Library of Congress Control Number: 2018942680

Published by:
Golden Antelope Press
715 E. McPherson
Kirksville, Missouri 63501

Available at:
Golden Antelope Press
715 E. McPherson
Kirksville, Missouri, 63501
Phone: (660) 665-0273
http://www.goldenantelope.com
Email: ndelmoni@gmail.com

For my mother and father

Acknowledgements

I want to thank my wife, Liz, Kathy Kennedy, Christine des Garennes, Andi Rogers, Greg Icenhower and Dan Mersch for their helpful feedback on many of the stories in this collection.

I want to thank Betsy and Neal Delmonico, who own and operate Golden Antelope Press, for being wonderful partners once again. This has included giving me the opportunity to work with two terrific college interns, Aura Martin and Mackenna Palazza, to help prepare and launch this book.

I also want to thank Maggie Toerner for creating the perfect cover illustration and Rusty Nelson for his superb graphic design work.

Finally, I want to extend grateful acknowledgement to the editors of the online literary magazines where the original version of many of these stories appeared: *101 Words*, *Flash Fiction Magazine*, *TWJ Magazine*, *Sick Lit Magazine*, *TreeHouse Arts*, *Friday Flash Fiction*, *formercactus*, *Edify Fiction*, *Sincerely Magazine*, and *Red Fez*.

Don Tassone

Contents

Preface

These days, we're all busy. But most people I know love to read. So I decided to create a collection of short stories for busy people. Many of the stories here can be read in about a minute. The longest might take half an hour.

At some point, I began to think of all these stories as a meal. Thus, the title, *Small Bites.* In keeping with that culinary theme, I've divided these stories into appetizers, entrees and desserts—to fit every taste and appetite.

An appetizer, of course, is a small dish, intended to stimulate your desire for more. It also usually hints at the main foods to come. I hope the 14 stories in this section will whet your appetite.

An entree is the main course. It's substantive and hearty. I hope you'll find the 12 longer stories in this section satisfying and memorable.

Desserts should be delicious, but not necessarily nutritious. They're sweet. They contain fat and sugar and should leave you with a sense of fullness. I hope the 14 stories in this section leave you feeling wonderfully full.

One of the entrees, "The Beauty Inside," is a sequel to a story in my first collection, *Get Back.* That story is called "The Beauty in Things." It's a love story. Many readers asked me to write a sequel. I am delighted to serve up this second course.

I hope you enjoy reading these stories as much as I enjoyed writing them.

Don Tassone
March 2018

Part I

Appetizers

Wild Dreams

His alarm went off precisely at six. So did his coffee maker and TV.

CNN was playing on the flatscreen in his kitchen. He scanned his email and Facebook as he sipped coffee and chewed on a breakfast bar. He had two more friend requests overnight. He accepted them both.

He grabbed his laptop and stepped down the hallway to his office, where he traded online all day. He took a break just before noon to run on his treadmill and down a protein shake for lunch.

At five, he decided to chat on Facebook with a handful of his now 464 friends. Then he ordered dinner from his favorite Chinese restaurant. A young man delivered it to his door. He took the bag from him and nodded. He had already paid and left a tip online.

He enjoyed chicken lo mein, egg rolls and hot oolong tea as he watched a movie on Netflix, relaxing in his recliner.

He was in bed by 10. He drifted off to sleep and dreamed, as usual, about living in the wild.

Ah

The old woman shuffled across the hard-packed earth until she found a large, smooth stone to sit on. She had arrived early to watch the sun rise over the sandstone spires of Angkor Wat.

Hundreds had gathered there in the morning mist. Their faces and dress told her that many had traveled from distant places.

All was silent. Then as the sun peeked from behind the ancient temple, she heard a sound. It arose from the crowd, even as it emerged from her own lips.

"Ah."

This, she thought, must be the sound of God being breathed into the new day.

Walk in the Grass

George and Jane met in a park, walking across the grass on a sunny day.

Now, five years later, it was time to start a family. For most young couples, this would be such a happy moment. But most young couples aren't on a spaceship, just beginning a 30-year odyssey to Pluto and back.

They had signed up for this adventure knowing their children and grandchildren would be born in space. They would all be pioneers. The idea had seemed so bold and exciting.

But now, watching Earth shrink in the distance, they wanted only to feel the soft grass beneath their feet.

My Father

Keeping an eye on his little boy, who was playing with some other children in the sand, the father watched at a distance.

He knew what was coming: two of the other boys, much bigger than his son, started yelling and shoving each other. Ready to intervene, the father stood up. But he stopped.

His son stepped into the fray. He extended his arms as if he were calming the seas and spoke in a low, measured voice. Gradually, the warring boys relaxed and began to play again.

Later, walking alongside his son, the father asked, "How'd you do that?"

The boy looked up and smiled.

"I learned from my father."

Bill Collector

It was a starter-home subdivision filled with 30-somethings.

All the houses were new except one. Herman lived there alone. He had been widowed before his young neighbors were even born. He took walks every day, but no one ever stopped to talk with him.

With budgets tight, most neighbors gathered to play cards on Friday nights.

"We didn't get an electric bill last month," Matt said. "They said it'd been paid in cash."

"Funny," said Lindsey. "Same thing with our water bill."

The young homeowners were busy. They never paid much attention to Herman, shuffling along the sidewalks, following the mailman.

Peace

Adnan looked up at the cross. Growing up in Syria, he had heard things about crosses which made him uneasy. He'd never set foot in a church.

Long before the present crisis, Germany had opened its borders to Turkish peoples. Growing up, Julia had had a few so-called Turks in her classes in school. But they knew little German and maintained their own customs, and she never got to know them personally.

Now, as Syrian refugees streamed into Germany, Julia wasn't sure she was up to the task she'd been assigned by her parish elders. The very idea of so many strangers flooding into her homeland made her anxious.

Adnan stared at the iron cross on the door before him. He remembered the stories from his homeland, and his heart was filled with fear.

But he knew what he must now do. With his wife and two young children huddled behind him, he reached out and pulled open the heavy, wooden door.

Julia stood waiting, just inside.

"*Salam*," she said, extending her hand.

"*Frieden*," he said, taking it.

On the Other Foot

Before the economy tanked, we got an hour for lunch. But then, there were three of us working there. It took three of us to shine all those shoes. We had customers non-stop from eight to five, Monday through Friday, and we did a pretty good business on Saturdays too.

Then the bottom fell out. Now customers trickle in, and it's just me shining. I feel lucky to still have a job. No more hour-long lunches, though. I can't be away that long anymore. I might miss a customer or two. So I either bring my lunch or run next door to grab something.

Today I forgot to pack a lunch and decided to run over to the burger joint across the street.

"May I help you, sir?" the man behind the counter asked.

"A cheeseburger, small fries and a small Coke," I said.

"For here or to go?"

"To go."

"Yes, sir," the man said, ringing up my order. "That'll be three dollars and thirty-nine cents."

His voice sounded familiar. I looked at the face beneath the blue cap into warm, brown eyes I hadn't seen in a while.

"Mr. Milligan?" I said.

He looked up at me and smiled.

"Hello, Sammy," he said, standing straighter and extending his hand.

8

I shook his hand and handed him a five, just as he had done to me so many times before, except he used to tuck the bill between his fingers.

The Wrong Track

The tall, well-groomed man in the navy blue suit slid his MetroCard through the card reader. The screen in the turnstile flashed green. He pushed against the aluminum bar with his thigh and stepped through the gate, toward the open door of the waiting subway car.

Only two more weeks of this, he thought. In two weeks, he would officially be a partner in the firm, he'd be living in his fabulous new place uptown, and a driver would be dropping him right in front of his office every morning and picking him up every night. He hoped to never ride the subway again.

He had grown to hate riding the subway. He hated the pungent odor of it. He hated the crowds. He hated the beggars with their crude cardboard signs and lame supplications. He hated the screech of the train cars coming to a stop. He hated the woman's robotic voice over the loudspeakers. He hated the hard plastic seats.

Most of all, he hated the passengers. Some were okay, the other business people, but he found most of them repulsive. He took the subway only because driving in the city was such a hassle and his office was too far to walk. He never told anyone for fear of what they might think of him. He couldn't wait to start telling everyone he had a driver.

Tonight he had to work late. At rush hour, the subway was usually packed. But now, as he got in, he noticed there was only one other passenger.

He sat down across from him, staying close to the doors. He looked like a punk who'd be in *The Fast and the Furious*. He was probably in his early twenties. He had a crew cut. His face was covered with stubble. He had two silver piercings along the top of each eyebrow. He wore black jeans, black boots with pointy toes and a white, skin-tight muscle shirt. Tattoos covered his arms and ran up his neck. All of them were green or blue except for one on each of his skinny biceps which read "Mom." Those two were red, each surrounded by the outline of a heart.

Mom, he thought. *This guy has a mom? If so, I wonder what she would think of her little boy if she could see him now. Sorry, mom*, he thought. *Your son's become a freak.*

He hated tattoos. He considered them barbaric and uncouth. He even had a personal rule against hiring anyone with even a hint of a tattoo showing.

And here, sitting across from him, was a guy covered with enough ink to fill a barrel. How grotesque. How could anyone do that to themselves? How could anyone think that was even the least bit attractive? *I hope it keeps him from ever getting a real job*, he thought. *I hope I never see a guy like this again. I can't wait to have my own driver.*

He was looking at a tattoo of a snake which ascended the young man's chest, from under his muscle shirt, and wound up around his neck. He was staring at the snake's forked tongue when he realized the young man was looking at him. The two of them made eye contact for a moment, but the man quickly looked away.

A minute later, he glanced back. The punk was staring at him. Now he began to feel anxious. *Maybe this guy wants to rob me*, he thought. *Maybe he's sizing me up. Maybe it's no coincidence that there's no one else in the car.*

The man looked down at his watch. He would arrive in one minute. *When we stop*, he thought, *I'll get out in a hurry, before this guy has a chance to make a move.*

As the train began to brake, he glanced up. The punk was still staring at him. The train hadn't quite stopped, but he grabbed the pole to his left, pulled himself up and swung around.

Just as the doors began to open, a series of shrill alarms blared from the intercom, like the warning sound a forklift makes when it's backing up. The man hadn't heard such a noise on the subway before, and he wondered what it meant. But he wasn't going to stick around to find out.

Just as he slid his right foot through the opening doors, he felt himself being jerked back.

"What the hell?" he cried out, stumbling backwards.

The young man had grabbed his suit coat and was pulling him back into the car.

"What's going on?" the man demanded, reeling around and tugging himself free of the young man's grip.

Then he heard the whoosh of a speeding train just beyond the half-opened doors behind him.

"It's a malfunction," the young man said. "We're on the wrong track."

The Run

He started running, not knowing whether he could make it. He had never run in the Grand Canyon.

He'd expected the trail to be more gradual. He didn't expect to see mountain lions, coyotes and snakes.

Halfway there, he ran out of water, and his calves began cramping. But he pushed through, focusing on the pines and junipers along the rim up ahead.

Just when he felt he had nothing left, he reached it.

"You did it!" proclaimed an avatar on the screen, pumping his little fists.

Yeah, he said to himself, stepping off the treadmill.

Tomorrow, Glacier National Park.

Friends

The boy stood astride his new bike at the end of his driveway. His friend spotted him and came over to check it out.

"Cool," he said. "What color is it?"

"Red."

"Looks orange to me."

"Are you nuts? It's red."

"Red? You're color-blind."

"You're full of crap."

"It's red."

"You're an idiot."

Without saying goodbye, his friend took off.

The boy got off his bike, walked it back into his garage and went inside his house.

A few minutes later, he got a text from his friend.

OK. It's red.

Wanna ride bikes?

Home

If only she could stay put. At this point, all she cared about was the safe delivery of her unborn child. And yet she knew they would all be in danger if they didn't leave soon.

The next morning, she and her husband packed what they needed for the journey and headed south on foot.

Given her condition, they walked slowly and rested often. At night, they either stayed with strangers who would take them in or slept under the stars.

After five days on the road, she could go no farther.

"The time is near," she said to her husband. "We need to find a place where I can have our baby."

He swung their bedrolls off his back and laid them on the grass under the shade of an oak tree. He helped her lie down and get comfortable, tucking his blanket under her head.

"I'll try to find a place nearby," he said, kissing her gently on the forehead. "I'll be back soon."

He ran to the first house he came upon and knocked on the door. He could hear someone inside, but no one answered, so he moved on.

About a quarter of a mile down the road, he came to another house. An old woman came to the door. She opened it, but only a crack.

He could barely see her face. She looked afraid. He told her his wife was about to give birth and asked if they could take shelter inside, but she said no and closed the door.

There were no other houses in sight, so he kept walking. Finally, he spotted a farmhouse far from the road, set back near a woods. He ran to it and knocked on the door. No one answered. Desperate, he pushed the door open and looked inside. A few pieces of broken furniture were strewn about. Otherwise, the place was empty. He guessed it had been ransacked.

He stepped back outside. In the breeze, he smelled manure. He walked around back and found a stable. The door was open. He looked inside. It was empty.

He hurried back to his wife and explained what he had found.

"I wish there were somewhere better," he said. "But at least it's tucked away. I think we'll be safe there."

He helped her to her feet. She clung to him as they made their way down the road.

That night, they slept in the stable. The next morning, she gave birth to a boy. Her husband wrapped him in his blanket.

The next day, hungry and low on food, he decided to go back to the old woman's house, where he had been two days before. Once again, she opened the door only a crack.

This time, he told her about the birth of his son and begged her for food.

"Wait here," she said, closing the door.

A few minutes later, she pulled the door ajar and, through the narrow opening, handed him something wrapped in paper.

"Thank you," he said. "I can pay you."

"No need," she replied. "It is my gift."

They were able to stay in the stable only a few more days. The thunder of violence was getting too close.

They gathered their things and, infant in tow, kept moving south. Finally, across the border, they found refuge among strangers.

He sat in a makeshift shelter next to his wife, watching her suckle their newborn son.

"I'm sorry it has to be this way," he said.

"What do you mean?" she asked.

"I wish we were home."

"Oh," she said, reaching out for his hand and smiling. "But we are."

The Cabin

As a boy, he used to venture out with his friends on Saturday mornings, escaping the safe and neat confines of their subdivision to explore the still wild woods nearby.

One Saturday morning, deep in the woods, they discovered a dilapidated log cabin. The only signs of life were vines snaking through holes in the chinking of the walls.

Large stones formed a step at the base of the door. Dared by his friends, the boy stepped up and yanked the door open.

That was the last Saturday the boys would leave the safe and neat confines of their subdivision.

It Pays to Listen

Every afternoon except Sunday, Bobby would fold 47 newspapers in thirds, slip rubber bands around them, stuff them into his saddlebags and set off on his bike.

He tossed papers onto the driveways of all his customers, except one, Mrs. Davis. She was old and lived alone. She insisted Bobby bring the paper to her front door.

She was often waiting there, eager to chat. Bobby was usually in a hurry, but he always took time to listen to whatever Mrs. Davis had to say.

Mrs. Davis wasn't a big tipper. But when she died, she left Bobby a small fortune.

Selfie

He was a strikingly handsome man.

He made a practice of having his picture taken wherever he went. Being a senior executive, when he traveled on business, there was always someone more junior who was quite happy to perform the task.

When he traveled with friends, they would hand waiters, waitresses and even passersby their cameras and iPhones so they could get in the shot.

Over the years, he collected thousands of pictures of himself. He kept them in albums.

Sometimes when he would look at them at home, alone, he wished he had someone to share them with.

Part II

Entrees

Who I Found in Angle Inlet

Angle Inlet is a secluded town, population 60. Technically, it's in Minnesota. But to get there, you have to go into Manitoba and then back south. Outside Alaska, it's the only place in the United States north of the 49th parallel.

Minnesota became a state in 1858. That's the year Jacques Bernard was born. He was born in Angle Inlet. There's a rumor he still lives there. I know that sounds crazy. But I'd heard that rumor all my life, and I had to find out for myself.

So I set out for Angle Inlet to see if I could find the oldest man on Earth.

#

I first heard the rumor as a boy, growing up in Minneapolis.

"That's right," my friend Greg said when we were about eight years old. "He was born in 1858."

I was too young to do the math in my head. But I knew my grandfather was born in 1920 and that he was now dead. I knew it was impossible for anyone born in the 1850s to still be alive.

"Bullshit," I said.

"Yeah, bullshit," said my friend Doug.

"How do you guys know it's not true?" asked Greg.

"Nobody could live that long," said Doug.

"Yeah," I said.

"Well, guess what?" Greg said. "Those guys in the Bible lived hundreds of years."

"That's a bunch of crap!" Doug said. "Those stories aren't really true."

"Yeah!" I said. "A bunch of crap!"

And so it went all through my childhood. Every once in a while, someone would say they'd heard yet another new rumor that a guy named Jacques Bernard, born before the Civil War, was living in a cabin in the woods in Angle Inlet.

By the time I turned 40, my life had become crowded and busy. I had a family, a wife and two kids. I had a big job, with global responsibility. I traveled a lot. Between email and social media, I was almost always online. And wherever I went, it seemed CNN was breaking in with dreadful news. My life had grown frantic, heavy, and rather predictable.

One evening, we were having dinner as a family, a rare feat anymore. My son, Ethan, mentioned that someone at school had told him about a very old man living in the woods in a place called Angle Inlet.

"What?" I asked.

"Yeah, Dad. His name is Jacques Bernard. He was born before the Civil War."

"That's impossible. He'd be 160 years old now," my wife said.

"I heard it too," my daughter, Emma, said.

I hadn't heard that rumor in a while. Maybe my life had gotten too busy or the din of my everyday existence had grown too loud. Now, hearing it again, from my children, made me think of my own childhood and how such a silly rumor had captivated my friends and me, long before the bombardment of the internet and non-stop news. Thinking about that made me long for a simpler time. It made me want to take a break from my serious, grown-up life and chase down a fanciful, childhood dream.

#

I left my home in Eden Prairie, a suburb of Minneapolis, for Angle Inlet on a Saturday morning in early July.

"Please stay in touch," said my wife, Melissa, sounding tentative.

"I will," I said. "I'll call you every day that I have cell reception."

"Okay," she said, giving me a big hug. "But I hate the idea that you might be out of touch."

"Don't worry. I'll be fine," I said, as I gave Emma and Ethan a kiss and a hug.

But in truth, I wasn't sure about this trip. I mean taking a week off of work to find a guy who was supposed to be older than my great, great grandfather, living in a part of the world so remote that most residents of the same state had never heard of it and so oddly situated that surveyors, mapmakers and government officials had trouble deciding which country it was in.

I must be going through some sort of a midlife crisis, I thought.

But I had to find out, once and for all, if the rumor was true. So I got in my car, waved goodbye to my family, and headed north on MN-89.

It took me nearly eight hours to reach the Canadian border. According to Google Maps, it should have taken me six. But every hour or so, I stopped to catch up on email and texts.

After clearing customs, I headed northeast along two different highways through the prairies of Manitoba. At some point, I lost cell reception. So I pulled over, pulled a map out of my glove box and spread it out on my passenger seat, the old-fashioned way.

Finally, I came to a sign that read "Welcome to the United States." In smaller type below, it said visitors must stop ahead at a place called Jim's Corner and report to customs.

Soon the highway became a bumpy, two-lane road. I spotted a small, wooden hut marked "Jim's Corner." I got out, opened the door and stepped inside. There in a booth was a videophone with two red buttons, one for visitors from Canada to call US Customs, the other for visitors from the US to call Canadian Customs.

I picked up the phone receiver and pressed the button for US Customs. A stern-looking woman appeared on the small screen in front of me. She asked me my name, where I was from and where I was heading. Then she asked me to hold up my passport.

"Enjoy your stay," she said clinically.

I got back in my car. Now the road turned from paved to gravel. A few minutes later, I spotted a small sign that read "Welcome to Angle Inlet, Pop. 60."

I looked around and saw a few small, wooden buildings: a post office, a school house, a church, a general store. There were no other cars and only a few people walking around. *This must be downtown Angle Inlet,* I thought.

I had booked a cabin at Young's Bay Resort, near the edge of the Lake of the Woods, dubbed "The Walleye Capital of the World." It was just a few minutes away. I checked in and put my gear in my cabin, which I was glad to learn had WiFi.

Across the street was a place called Jerry's Bar and Restaurant. It was early evening, and I was hungry. I called Melissa to let her know I'd arrived, then walked across the street to get something to eat.

Jerry's was a long, gray, wood building. Hanging between posts along the front porch were two big red and white banners with "Budweiser" along the top and "Welcome Fishermen" along the bottom. I walked up the steps, opened the door and went inside.

The place was packed with guys wearing caps and fishing vests. Country music was blasting. Cigarette smoke hung thick in the air. On a widescreen TV, the Twins were playing the Reds. I didn't see an open table, so I took a seat at the bar.

"What can I get ya, buddy?" the bartender asked.

"Hi," I said. "I'll start with a Budweiser. And could I see a menu?"

"Menu?"

"Yeah."

He looked down the bar at the other bartender.

"Hey, Debbie! You got a menu?"

"What?" she asked, squinting her eyes through the smoke from her cigarette.

"A menu!"

"Yeah. Hang on," she said in a gravelly voice.

She stepped down to the end of the bar, near a window into the kitchen, and picked up what looked like a small, laminated sheet of paper. She stepped down our way and handed it to my bartender.

"Thanks," he said, as Debbie squinted at me and took a drag from her cigarette.

"Here you go," my bartender said, handing me the menu.

"Thanks."

I looked down at the menu. It was indeed a laminated sheet of paper, with a limited selection, printed by hand: hamburger, cheeseburger, fish sandwich, french fries, coleslaw, soup of the day and vegetable medley (seasonal).

A bowl of vegetable soup sounded good.

"What's your soup today?"

"Chili."

"How about the vegetable medley?"

"It's not in season yet."

"Okay. I guess I'll have a cheeseburger, french fries and coleslaw."

"Comin' right up," he said, taking the menu.

He walked over to the window into the kitchen and yelled, "The special!" Then he grabbed a bottle of Bud, popped the top and sat it down in front of me. He grabbed beers for a couple of other guys at the bar, then came back down to me.

"First time in?" he asked.

"Yeah," I said. "It's my first time to Angle Inlet."

"Here to do some fishing?"

"No, not really."

"Camping?"

"No, I've come up here from downstate, looking for somebody."

"Really? Who are you looking for, if you don't mind me asking."

"I'm looking for a man named Jacques Bernard."

He looked at me, smiled a half smile and blew air out of his nostrils.

"You mean the oldest man on Earth?"

"Yeah! Do you know him?"

"I know a guy named Jacques Bernard. But he's not the oldest man on Earth."

"How old would you say he is?"

"I'd say he's around 80."

Rumors morph, I thought. *It's the nature of rumors. Maybe there's an old guy up here named Jacques Bernard whose great, great grandfather was born in 1858, or something like that. I must be crazy,* I thought. *And this bartender must think I'm crazy.*

"Does he live around here?" I asked, just trying to make polite conversation.

"Well, he lives somewhere around here. I don't know where, exactly. Somewhere out in the state forest."

"How do you know him?" I asked, now wondering if I was being played.

"He comes in here, two or three times a year. He sells us vegetables he grows on his land out there. You know, the vegetables for our medley."

Well, at least he knows a guy named Jacques Bernard, I thought.

"Oh, I see."

"Why are you looking for him?"

"Well, it might sound crazy. But I've heard that rumor about him all my life, and I decided to take a week off work and come up here and find out once and for all."

"Well, I'm sorry to tell you this, but I think you're wasting your time."

"Why is that?"

"You're not going to find him. And you're not the first fella who's come up here looking for him either."

"Food's up!" someone yelled from the kitchen.

"I'll be right back," the bartender said.

He came back and sat my food down on the bar.

"Ketchup?"

"Yes, please."

"Debbie! Bottle of ketchup!"

"Anything else?" Debbie said sarcastically.

"Yeah," Dave said. "While you're at it, how about a napkin and some silverware too?"

Debbie grabbed a bottle of ketchup, a napkin and a fork from under the bar.

"Here you go, mister," she said, her cigarette bouncing up and down as she spoke.

"Thanks."

I opened the bottle and shook some ketchup onto my plate.

"I don't think I caught your name, young fella," the bartender said.

"My name is Jason," I said, extending my hand. "Jason Peterson."

He took my hand. His skin felt like leather.

"Dave. Dave Swanson."

"Good to meet you," I said.

"Likewise."

"So this guy, Bernard. He lives in a forest?"

"Yeah, in the Northwest Angle State Forest, just south of here."

"But you're not sure where?"

"No, and there's a lot of land out there."

"Is there a trail into the forest?"

"Yeah. There are several trails in. But you're wasting your time if you think you're ever going to find him there. You'd be better off waiting until he brings us those vegetables."

"When will that be?"

"About two weeks."

"Well, I need to be home by Friday."

"Too bad."

"How far do each of those trails go?"

"I don't know for sure. I'd say about 10 miles. It's a big forest."

"How would I get to those trails?"

"Well, you'd drive back down the main road you came in on. A few miles down the road, you'll see the first trailhead on your left."

"How about the other trailheads?"

"They're farther down the road. Those trails are about a mile apart."

"So there's just three trails into the forest?"

"Well, there's another trail beyond those three. But you can't hike it."

"Why not?"

"It's on Red Lake Indian land. It's off limits to people like you and me."

"Got it."

"Another Bud?"

"Why not? I'm on vacation."

#

I got up early the next morning, put on hiking clothes and drove into town to buy some food for the week. My cabin was equipped with a full kitchen. When I got back, I made myself a hearty breakfast.

Then I started packing for my hike. I grabbed my backpack and threw in a pair of socks, a T-shirt, a poncho, a compass, a flashlight, bug spray, bear spray, a water filter, a first aid kit and a couple of water bottles. Then I made a couple of ham and cheese sandwiches and stuffed them, a couple of granola bars and an apple in the bag too.

I sat down and sent a text message to Melissa to let her know I'd be hiking all day, probably out of cell phone range, and that I'd call her that night.

I slipped my backpack on to try it out. It was light. I walked to my car and slid my pack onto the back seat.

I looked over at the lake. I could see a bunch of fishing boats on the water. A few guys were slipping their boats out of a marina. Someone was backing a boat down a ramp into the water. *No wonder no one knows where Jacques Bernard lives*, I thought. *Angle Inlet is about fishing. Everybody here is on the water, not in the woods.*

I drove through town and back out on the main road. A few miles later, I saw a trailhead at the edge of the woods, just as Dave had said. I parked my car across the road. I grabbed my backpack, slipped it on and hit the trail.

It was mid-morning. I figured I'd hike for about three hours, then head back. That way, I'd be sure to get back before dark. I also figured six hours of hiking was about all I could handle. I ran on a treadmill a few times a week, but I was hardly in great shape. I hoped my 40-year-old body was up to the task.

Thankfully, the terrain was pretty flat, and the trail was clear. The forest was thick with spruces and birch trees, cedars and pines. I saw lots of birds, squirrels and deer. At one point, I heard a noise through the trees which I thought was a deer. It turned out to be a moose. I had heard moose could be dangerous. I was ready to climb a tree. But the moose just looked at me and moved on.

It was getting hot. I made sure I stay hydrated. By noon, I had drunk both bottles of water. I stopped at a creek and used my filter to refill my water bottles. I sat on a rock overlooking a small waterfall and ate a sandwich, a granola bar and an apple for lunch.

I pulled out my cell phone. Sure enough, no coverage. I thought about my family. I hoped they were all right. I thought about the emails that must be piling up in my inbox and the projects that would be waiting for me at work. I wondered what was going on the world. I missed Google News.

I hiked on, deeper into the forest. Dave had said these trails go for about 10 miles. If the terrain stayed flat and the trails stayed clear, I figured I could hike 10 miles in a few hours. Therefore, if Dave was right, I should be able to cover all three trails in three days.

I kept hiking. I saw another moose but no people. I knew finding Jacques Bernard was a long shot. But I thought I might at least see other hikers. I guessed they were all fishing.

I wasn't used to being alone. At work, I was constantly interacting with other people, in person, by phone or online. It felt strange to be alone. I felt a bit off-balance. I missed being plugged in.

I looked at my watch. I'd been hiking for a little more than three hours. I decided to head back.

On my way back, I started thinking about work again. Once again, I began to wonder if this trip was such a good idea. I mean there was virtually no way I was going to find Jacques Bernard, and I was burning a week of my vacation. I had to be going through a mid-life crisis.

When I got back to my cabin, I showered, changed clothes and called Melissa. I checked a few email messages and scanned the news online. I was pretty tired and didn't feel like fixing dinner for myself. So I walked over to Jerry's.

Once again, the place was packed with fishermen, so I sat at the bar. I didn't see Dave tonight. Debbie was on duty. I ordered a Budweiser and the special.

"Sure thing, darlin," Debbie said, the tip of her cigarette affixed to her bottom lip.

#

My second day of hiking, on the second trail, was much the same as my first, except today I passed a few hikers. I asked if they'd seen any cabins or anyone living in the woods. They said no.

I had a growing sense this was a wild goose chase. Yet I felt less regret about being there. As I had gone through my email the night before and scanned it again that morning, I had resisted responding to any of my messages. I knew that responding would send a bad signal to my employees about how they should be spending *their* vacations. More than that, though, I realized that I really didn't need to respond. Either someone else would take care of the urgent stuff or it could wait until I got back. For the first time in years, I didn't simply react. It felt good.

Just like the day before, I found a stream and stopped for lunch. The day before, I had gotten back well before dark. So I decided to push it a little and hike for four hours before turning around, assuming the trail went that far. I found out it did.

As I hiked back, I began to feel tired. When I reached the stream where I'd had lunch, I decided to lie down on a bed of pine needles and take a little nap, using my knapsack as a pillow. I seldom took naps back home. I never seemed to have the time. Now, resting, listening to my body, feeling the warm earth beneath me, breathing in the fragrance of pine, felt good.

When I got back to my cabin, I called Melissa. But I decided not to check email or go online at all. Instead, I took a shower and walked over to Jerry's for dinner again.

Dave was tending bar again. He asked if I'd seen Jacques Bernard yet. I told him no. He laughed and said I told you so.

We started talking about our families. We must have talked for an hour. Then I went back to my cabin and fell into a deep sleep.

#

The next day, I made myself a big breakfast and took off for the third trail. I did not check email before I left.

I got an early start and decided to push it today, to see if I could hike five hours out and five back. I didn't know if the forest extended that far. But I figured this might be my last chance to find Jacques Bernard, and I wanted to give it my all.

It was early afternoon. I'd been hiking for nearly five hours. I was just about to turn around when, up ahead to my left, I thought I saw a moose through the trees. I stopped. I squinted to get a better look. Whatever it was, it was big, and it wasn't moving. I kept walking on the trail. As I got closer to the object, I realized it was a cabin.

My heart was beating fast and hard. Could I have found him? I came to a thin, overgrown trail leading to the cabin. I took a deep breath and stepped onto it.

I tried to be quiet, but twigs snapped beneath my feet. The front door of the cabin creaked open. I froze.

"Who's there?" came a disembodied voice from inside.

I was afraid. I didn't know what to say.

"I said, who's there?"

A figure appeared at the door, a man of slight build, with long white hair and a long beard, wearing a brown shirt and overalls. He stepped out onto the porch. His hands hung empty at his sides.

"My name," I said in a trembling voice, "is Jason Peterson."

"What do you want, Jason Peterson?"

"I'm looking for a man named Jacques Bernard."

The old man stepped over to a rocking chair on the porch and sat down.

"Then I suppose you found him," he said.

I couldn't move. I remembered my friend Greg all those years ago talking about the old men in the Bible living hundreds of years. I wasn't close enough to see how old this guy might be, but I wasn't sure I was welcome to come any closer.

"You just going to stand there all day, young man?"

Well, this is it, I thought. The moment of reckoning. I stepped forward on the trail until I was just short of the steps to his porch.

"Come on up," the old man said. "I don't bite."

Trying my best not to look afraid, I grabbed the railing and climbed the steps. When I reached the porch, the old man stood up and extended his hand.

"Jacques Bernard," he said.

"Jason Peterson," I said, taking his hand. It felt bony and frail.

"Pull up that chair over there," he said nodding toward the end of the porch and sitting back down in his rocker. "It's a little dusty, but still plenty sturdy, I think."

I picked up the chair and put it down about 10 feet away from him. Then I sat down.

Now I got a better look. His hair was wispy, his face a labyrinth of wrinkles, and his clothes hung on him like a scarecrow. But his eyes were green and bright. I remember thinking he had the eyes of a child.

"So why are you out here, looking for me?" he asked, smiling. He was missing a good number of teeth.

"Well, Mr. Bernard, I've heard a rumor about you for a very long time."

"Is that right? What kind of rumor?"

"Well, I know it sounds crazy. But all my life I've heard a rumor that you're the oldest man on Earth."

"The oldest man on Earth, huh? Well, I have been slowing down a bit lately," he chuckled.

"Mr. Bernard, if you don't mind me asking, how old are you?"

"How old am I? Well, let's see. My arithmetic is getting a little rusty."

"Well, what year were you born?"

"That I know, Mr. Peterson. I was born in 1858."

I expected him to say something else. Maybe like he was off by 80 years. But he just sat there, with a small smile, gently rocking.

"Did you say 1858?"

"That's right. I was born right here in 1858."

"So that would mean you're 159 years old."

"I reckon so."

"But that's impossible!"

"Maybe for you. Maybe for most folks. But not for me."

"What do you mean?"

"Do you mean how is it that I could live this long?"

"Well, yes."

"Come with me," he said, slowly pushing himself up on the arms of his chair. "I'll show you."

He turned around, pulled open the door to his cabin and shuffled inside. I got up and followed him.

The cabin was one big room, though there was a ladder ascending into an opening in the ceiling, so I assumed there was also a loft of some sort. There was a bed in one corner. There was a table with four chairs around it and an oil lamp on top. There was an open-faced cabinet in the corner near the table. In it were a few dishes, pots and pans, utensils and ceramic mugs. Three rocking chairs ringed the stone fireplace, which had a brown rug in front of it. Embers glowed in the fireplace, and I could smell smoke. Inside the hearth was a big, black pot, suspended by an iron arm anchored into the stone. Two kerosene lanterns hung from wooden rods extending from the walls. There was a bookcase against one wall, filled with books. Several windows made of thick glass let in scattered light. I saw no appliances or any sign of electricity.

"Back here, Mr. Peterson," the old man said, opening a back door and stepping through it.

I followed him out onto a back porch. Just beyond it was a clearing in the woods, about the size of a small backyard in suburbia, where I lived. It was filled with light green meadow grass. In the center of the grass was a large, rectangular garden.

Tools of all sorts—a shovel, a spade, a mattock, a hoe, a bow saw, a rake—were neatly arranged along the back porch, leaning against the wall of the cabin.

"Let me show you my garden," the old man said, descending two steps, holding tight to the wooden railing.

I followed him down the steps and out onto a dirt path which led to the garden. The old man walked slowly, but without assistance. When he got to the edge of the garden, he stopped and put his hands on his hips. I stood next to him.

"Here, Mr. Peterson," he said, nodding toward dozens of neat rows of vegetables. "Here is your answer."

When I was growing up, my mother had kept a vegetable garden in our backyard. I used to help her tend it. We grew carrots, beans, tomatoes, lettuce, squash, peppers and corn. I saw all these here. This garden was bigger than my mother's. But the vegetables looked the same.

"I don't understand," I said. "This garden is the reason for your longevity?"

"That's right," the old man said.

He stepped carefully between two rows of carrots, toward the center of the garden.

"Come," he said, motioning for me to follow him.

He took a few more small steps, then stopped. He bent down slowly, his knees cracking. He grabbed the leafy end of a carrot and yanked it up.

"Here you go, Mr. Peterson," he said, standing up and handing me the carrot.

"Thank you."

"You're welcome. Notice anything special about that carrot?"

I examined it, turning it over in my hands. I held it up to my nose and sniffed it.

"No, I don't," I said. "It seems like an ordinary carrot to me."

"Oh, but it's not! There are no other carrots like this grown anywhere in the world."

"What do you mean?"

"This carrot is the result of hundreds of years of cross-breeding. Part of it comes from the Red Lake Indians. Part of it comes from Southwestern France, where my parents were born. Part of it comes from Quebec, where they lived before settling here."

"Interesting," I said. "But it still looks like an ordinary carrot to me."

"And yet, Mr. Peterson, it is an extraordinary carrot."

"With respect, Mr. Bernard. How so?"

The old man turned and looked me in the eye.

"If you eat enough of this carrot, Mr. Peterson, or any of the vegetables grown in this garden, you will double your lifespan."

I blinked in disbelief.

"How do you know?"

"Let me show you something, Mr. Peterson," the old man said. "Follow me."

He carefully stepped back out of the garden and made his way through the meadow grass, toward the back of the clearing. I followed him. As we neared the edge of the grass, I noticed a stream. When we were almost to the stream, I saw two large rocks. Something was etched in each of them.

"Here, Mr. Peterson. Take a look."

I stepped closer to the rocks. On the first one was etched: *Philippe Bernard, 1831-1970*. On the other: *Josephine Bernard, 1833-1979*.

I couldn't believe my eyes.

"These stones mark the graves of my parents."

I felt dizzy. I took a deep breath.

"Are you okay?" he asked.

"Yes," I said. "Mr. Bernard, would you like to talk?"

We went back to his cabin and talked for the rest of that afternoon. He told me about his life. He told me about his first memories, there in the Northwest Angle, long before Angle Inlet was established.

He was an only child. As a boy, his parents used to take him to Fort St. Charles. It was more than a fort. It was a settlement, where people lived, met and traded. The fort itself was built by the French in the 1700s. But by the time Jacques was born, the British had taken over. More people in the area spoke English than French. Jacques grew up learning both languages.

His parents lived a simple life in the Northwest Angle, cultivating and tending their garden and fishing in the stream and, occasionally, the Lake of the Woods. Like Jacques, they made their livelihood by selling vegetables.

Jacques' father had a horse. Several times a year, he would ride it to nearby towns to sell his vegetables and a buy a few things. When Jacques was about 10, his father began taking him along. Jacques told me he saw a telephone and an electric light bulb when they were still relatively new inventions.

"What was that like?" I asked.

"I had mixed feelings," he said. "Part of me was astonished, of course. But part of me wondered how these things would change my life. I couldn't imagine talking to someone in another city, for example. It made me worry whether I would still appreciate where I lived. My life was simple. I knew that. I wasn't opposed to technology. But I had grown used to the slow pace of my life, to rising with the sun and feeling the earth in my hands. When I saw a car for the first time, part of me was in awe. But part of me felt sorry for the driver because he could no longer feel the earth beneath his feet. When I first heard a radio, I had a hard time imagining listening to someone's voice without seeing their face and not being able to talk with them. And television? Well, I just found that silly. I've been going into Angle Inlet for years to sell my vegetables. I've seen computers and cell phones there. The last few years I've been going into town, everybody's been too busy talking or typing on their phones to talk with me."

"We've all gotten pretty busy, I'm afraid."

He simply nodded.

"Did you ever think about moving away?" I asked.

"Oh, sure. Lots of times. But my parents depended on me. And like I said, I was happy here. It might seem simple to you, but I love tending this garden. I love to fish. I love the woods. I love to read. My mother taught me to read, and my father bought me lots of books. I read a lot. Every time I go into town, I buy a new book. I read the newspaper when I go into town too. It keeps me current."

"Do you ever get bored?"

"No, I don't. A long time ago, I learned not to think much about tomorrow, to just be thankful for today. Every morning when I wake up, I thank God for the new day. Every day, I walk in the woods. The trees, the animals, the rocks and streams, they're my friends. I swear the squirrels come out to greet me. Every day, I thank God for these woods. They're teeming with life, and they change all the time. There's something new to see every day."

I remembered playing in the woods near my house when I was a boy. I too loved the woods. How I missed those days.

"Were you ever married?" I asked.

"No. I met a girl once down in Grand Marais. I was there with my father. Her name was Anna. I liked her, and I actually went back to see her again. I rode my father's horse. I guess I was about 20. But all she talked about was wanting to move to the big city. I had no interest in that. So I knew I couldn't make her happy. I never saw her again. I like women, just never married one."

"That's fair," I said, smiling. "Mr. Bernard, you are, by any measure, an extraordinary man. You've seen more change than anyone on Earth. May I ask you something?"

"Of course."

"Is life getting better? I mean do you think the world is improving?"

He smiled and gently stroked his beard along the right side of his face with his fingertips. He looked over my shoulder, a faraway look, as if he were somewhere else. Then his gaze came back to me, and he looked me squarely in the eye.

"Do you know," he said, "I never had a real conversation with my father, not about the big things anyway. I'm not sure why. He just didn't seem interested in talking much. But he loved to listen. He bought me books. And not just any books. Take a look over there on those bookshelves, Mr. Peterson. You'll find Shakespeare, Tolstoy, Proust, Dickens, Hugo, Hawthorne, Thoreau, Whitman, Twain, Joyce, Hemingway, Faulkner, de Saint-Exupery, Frost and the King James Bible. My father knew all those books by heart. But he didn't know how to read. My mother and I read to him. My father lived and died in this little place. But he was a man of the world. I think the world is getting better, Mr. Peterson, because it's getting smaller. These days, anyone can become a person of the world. I just hope we don't forget the small things — the joy of walking in the woods, the wonder of watching a storm move in, the satisfaction of watching a garden grow. I hope people don't forget how to listen to one another."

He paused and smiled.

"What about you, Mr. Peterson?" he asked, folding his hands in front of him on the table and leaning forward slightly. "Tell me about your life."

I blinked, trying to absorb what he had just shared. Suddenly, my life seemed so superficial and boring.

"Well," I stammered, "I'm married. My wife and I have two kids, a boy and a girl, ten and eight. I live in Eden Prairie."

"Where's that?"

"Near Minneapolis."

"Oh."

"I work for a big software company. Do you know what software is, Mr. Peterson?"

"I'm familiar," he said with a grin.

"I'm a vice president there, in charge of new business development."

"Sounds like a pretty big job."

"It is. Some days, to be honest, maybe a little too big. I work nearly every day. I travel a lot. And I see my wife and kids less and less."

"Not good," he said.

"No. Not good at all."

"Do you have a cell phone?"

"Yeah."

"Doesn't work out here, does it?"

"No, it doesn't."

"How does that make you feel?"

"To be honest, I'm beginning to get used to it. I've been hiking out here in the forest for three days, and I'm beginning to get used to being out of touch."

"You mean you don't miss all that software stuff?"

"Not at all."

"What do you miss, Mr. Peterson?"

"I miss my wife and kids."

"Are you hungry?"

"Yeah. I guess I am getting hungry."

"You know, you'll never make it back to Angle Inlet tonight before dark."

"I guess you're right."

"You're welcome to stay here."

"I'd be glad to, Mr. Bernard. If it wouldn't be an inconvenience."

"No trouble at all. You can sleep in my old bed up in the loft."

"Mr. Bernard, do you mind if I ask you something?"

"Go right ahead."

"Have you ever told anybody the things you've told me today?"

"No, I haven't."

"Why not?"

"It's simple, Mr. Peterson. First, when I go into town, everybody is interested in my vegetables. But they're all too busy to ask about me. To be honest, despite our conversation today, small talk is not my strong suit. Second, you're the first person who's ever visited me here."

"You're kidding. The first?"

"Yep."

"I wonder why. Hasn't anybody ever come by here?"

"Oh, I see hikers out here from time to time. But they never stop. Only you have ever walked up to my cabin."

"I'm glad I did."

"Me too."

We went back out on the back porch. He handed me a fishing pole and a small, wooden box filled with dirt. We walked through the meadow grass to the stream. He took the fishing pole and the box from me. He stuck his fingers into the dirt and pulled out a worm. He baited his hook and threw his line into a pool, shaded by trees. A few minutes later, he pulled in a nice-sized trout.

"This should be enough for the two of us for dinner," he said. "Along with some vegetables, of course."

We stopped in the garden on the way back to his cabin and picked a variety of vegetables. It reminded me of spending time with my mother in her garden. I untucked my shirt and used my front shirttail to carry the vegetables. It was something my mother had taught me when I was a kid.

"Clever," the old man said.

When we got back to the cabin, he asked me to go down to the stream to get a bucket of water so he could wash the vegetables and we could wash our hands and have fresh water to drink with dinner.

"And pick some blackberries while you're there," he said. "You'll see berry bushes down by the stream. We'll have black-berries for dessert."

By the time I got back, he'd cleaned the fish and was frying it in a big pan, which sat on an iron grate over a low fire in the fireplace. I helped him clean and cut up the vegetables, which he added to the frying pan.

Over dinner, I asked, "Does this mean I'm going to live to be as old as you?"

He laughed.

"Not yet. This is only one helping. I've been eating these vegetables all my life. I'm not sure how many you'll have to eat to double your lifespan. But I know it's a lot more than a helping or two. Otherwise, a lot of people in Angle Inlet, and the people passing through there, would be my age!"

After dinner, we talked by the fire. He told me how it was to hear about American boys dying in Europe in the first world war and how his parents simply couldn't believe him when he told them astronauts had walked on the moon. I told him about my travels around the world and how Apple introduces a new iPhone every year and how people line up to buy them.

We shared stories about our earliest memories growing up, about our parents tucking us into bed at night, about skipping flat stones on a pond, about sleeping under the stars in the summer.

"I guess some things don't change," he chuckled.

As I climbed the ladder to the loft to go to bed, holding my flashlight in my teeth, I thought of Melissa and how I wouldn't be able to call her that night. I had told her cell reception might be spotty, even in Angle Inlet. I hoped she wouldn't worry.

I said goodbye to Mr. Bernard after breakfast the next morning. I'd given him a granola bar, the first he'd ever tried. He liked it.

He insisted I take a burlap sack full of vegetables. I put them into my backpack with extra care.

"You know," he said, "it's not just those vegetables that have made me grow so old."

"What do you mean?"

"I think there's another reason too."

"What's that?"

"Except for a few times when I was being chased by wild animals, I don't go fast. I go at my own pace. I've never owned a car or a radio or a TV or a telephone or a computer. I don't own anything that would make me go faster than I want to go. I wake up when the sun rises and go to sleep when it sets. Somehow, life slows down when you live at your own pace. You should try it, Mr. Peterson."

"I will," I said.

"Good," he said, extending his hand.

"Thank you," I said, taking it.

As we walked onto the front porch, I turned to him.

"Mr. Bernard, I do have one last question."

"What's that?"

"There must have been a lot of other hikers out this way over the years. Why do you think I was the first one who stopped?"

"Well, let me ask you, Mr. Peterson. Why did you come out here?"

"I was chasing a rumor, I guess. I needed to settle a question that had been on my mind for as long as I can remember. I just had to find out if you really exist."

"So you were curious."

"Yeah."

"Well, there's your answer, Mr. Peterson. People don't discover things because they follow the same path everyone else is on. They discover things because they're curious."

He sat down in his rocking chair.

"The world is still being created, Mr. Peterson," he said, his green eyes sparkling. "You and I are still being created. Stay curious. It's amazing what you'll find."

"Thank you, Mr. Bernard. I will."

As I descended his steps and started walking away, he said, "I suppose you'll be telling people about me."

"Only if you want me to."

"It's up to you."

"I'll think about it. I'm not sure anyone would believe me."

"Take care of yourself, Mr. Peterson. Your family too. Don't forget to slow down a bit."

#

When I got home, the vegetables were still fresh enough to eat. But I didn't eat them or give them to anyone. Instead, I dried them. I'm keeping the seeds to plant in the spring. Last fall, I dug a garden in my backyard. Emma and Ethan helped.

Now I am waiting. I am waiting for spring. The snow outside is nearly a foot deep. I used to use a snowblower at the first sign of snow to keep my driveway clean. Now Ethan and I shovel a path to the mailbox. Usually, a snowball fight breaks out.

I've been working from home a few days a week. Melissa and I don't go out as much. We've been spending much more time together as a family. Sometimes, we take walks in the woods.

I'm slowing down, spending more time with people and less time online. I walk every day, just to feel the earth beneath my feet. I started reading books again. I'm learning French. And I feel grateful for who I found in Angle Inlet.

The Moon and the Birds

Helen tucked the pillow behind her head, sat upright in bed and wondered what day it was.

She knew she should have sold the farm years ago and that by now she should be living in a retirement center or someplace where people could take care of her. But she kept putting it off, and there was no one around to help make it happen.

Someone from church still brought food for her once a week. But lately she was having a hard time fixing it, and she didn't have much of an appetite anyway. Some days, she simply stayed in bed. She was too weak to get out.

For a moment, she thought about watching TV. But she found the news too depressing. She considered reading, but lately she was having a hard time seeing the words, and her hands were too shaky to hold a book.

She looked over at the framed pictures on her nightstand, photos of her husband, Charlie, and her children, Michael and Susan. How she wished they were there with her now.

How she wished Charlie were there to kiss her good morning, as he always did before leaving to work in the fields or tend to the animals. Oh, to feel his lips on her cheek or hear him whisper "I love you."

It had been more than 10 years since he passed. And she hadn't had the strength to visit his grave near the woods for nearly three weeks now. She missed him.

Thinking of Charlie always made her think of the moon. When they were young, he had courted her under the moon. They danced by its light. He proposed to her under a full moon. When their kids were little, after they'd put them to bed, Charlie and Helen would sit together on the swing on the back porch and look up at the moon. And when their kids left home, they would cuddle in that same swing, like young lovers, gently rocking under the light of the moon.

"Gaze at it, Helen," he would tell her. "Let it draw you in. The moon is eternal. If you let yourself be drawn in, you too will live forever."

She would smile at him when he would talk that way. But he didn't mind. He was sure he was right. He claimed he could feel the moon's gravitational pull. He claimed he could feel the moon drawing him toward heaven.

If Charlie had a thing for the moon, Michael and Susan had a thing for birds. Helen didn't know where Charlie got his ideas about the moon. But she felt responsible for the way her children felt about birds.

When they were little, she would take them out into the fields. There they would spot cardinals, orioles, whippoorwills, yellow-headed blackbirds, barn swallows, robins, gold finches, wrens, blue jays, sparrows, hawks and black-capped chickadees. Whenever her children saw a bird, they would stop and study it and listen intently. They were captivated by birds. They learned all their names and spent hours practicing how to mimic their songs.

They got so good at it that sometimes Helen would look out the kitchen window, hearing some bird, only to find Michael or Susan, crouching in the bushes, whistling, tweeting or chirping. Of course, they were watching for her the whole time, and they would laugh when she saw them hiding, delighted that they had fooled her. It was a game they played all the while they were growing up.

Her memories of that time were so real that sometimes when Helen would hear birds singing through her open bedroom window, she would think Michael and Susan had come home to visit. And sometimes when she would see the moon through the curtains, she would think Charlie was sitting next to her on the porch swing.

Tonight she felt so tired. She hadn't done a thing all day, not even left her bed. She had simply lain there, thinking about her husband and her children, missing them, loving them, longing to be with them again.

Through her open window, she heard two birds singing together. A sparrow and a wren, she thought. Funny, she had never heard them singing together before, least of all at night.

Then she looked up and saw a harvest moon, so large in the sky that she felt she could reach out and touch it.

Helen smiled and closed her eyes. She saw the faces of her husband and children. They looked so happy to see her.

Charlie extended his hand and, without words, asked her to dance. Michael and Susan were running toward her, through the moonlit fields, laughing and calling her name. Birds, all the birds of their childhood, glided around them, guiding their way.

Helen took Charlie's hand, and they danced in the moonlight. Then she knelt down and gathered her children in, as birds filled the air with a song of sweet communion.

One Floor Up

It began in an elevator.

It was just after noon on a Wednesday. I was on my way to the cafeteria. It was only three floors up. Normally, I would've taken the stairs. But I was in a hurry, just grabbing a sandwich to eat at my desk.

The elevator stopped at eight. You were standing there alone, holding a book.

"Ten, please," you said softly, as you stepped inside. As you turned around, you saw the button was already lit. "Never mind," you added, with a small laugh.

You were standing right in front of me. Under the bright ceiling lights, I noticed the red in your chestnut brown hair as well as a few strands of gray.

The doors opened at nine. Several more people got in. You took a step back, and your left heel came down hard on the toe of my left shoe.

"Uggh!"

You wheeled around.

"Oh, I'm so sorry!" you exclaimed.

Turning around that way just as the elevator started ascending again threw you off balance. Instinctively, I grabbed your upper arms from behind and steadied you.

"It's okay," I said. "I'm fine."

You faced forward and said nothing. I imagined you were embarrassed.

The doors opened, and everyone got out. I walked over to the deli counter. Out of the corner of my eye, I could see you heading to the salad bar.

As I stood in line, I watched you place a plate, some silverware, a napkin and your book on a tray and assemble your salad. You were wearing low-heeled pumps. No wonder my left foot was throbbing.

You stepped over to the drink station. I noticed your toned calf muscles and slender waist. You dispensed Diet Pepsi over ice into a tall glass.

You got in line for the cashier. You paid, stopped for some salad dressing and walked into the dining room alone.

I grabbed my sandwich and a drink and headed back to my office. As the elevator passed the eighth floor, I wondered if you worked there.

#

You were at least 10 years my senior. But I couldn't stop thinking about you. I wanted to see you again.

I wondered if you went to the cafeteria for lunch every day. I took a chance. Just after noon the next day, I got on the elevator. Again, it stopped at eight. And again, there you were.

Once again, you were holding a book. Once again, you stood right in front of me. And once again, the doors opened at nine, and several more people got in.

This time, you were careful to avoid my toes. But a large man backed into you, pushing you hard against me and forcing me against the back wall. Instinctively, I put my hands on the sides of your waist to keep you from pressing into me.

"I'm sorry," I said.

"It's okay," you said, lightly squeezing my left hand. "You probably kept me from stepping on your other foot."

Your hair smelled like flowers. I looked down at your left hand and noticed you weren't wearing a ring.

The doors opened at 10. Everyone got out. You glanced over your shoulder and smiled. Your eyes were honey-brown.

I waited in line for a sandwich and watched as you once again got a salad and walked into the dining room alone.

#

It was Friday. Everyone in my office dresses down on Friday. Some even wear jeans. But today I wore a suit, without a tie.

All morning, I kept checking the clock. I couldn't wait for lunchtime. A few minutes after noon, I got into the elevator. I prayed that the doors would open at eight.

They did. And there you were.

Today you were wearing a sleeveless red dress and holding a small silver purse. You were looking at the spot where I always stand. When you saw me, you smiled.

"Hello again," you said.

"Hello," I smiled.

This time, you stepped in and pivoted just before you got to me, your back against the outside wall. We were at right angles. You glanced up at my face. I held your gaze for a moment. Then you looked down.

I couldn't take my eyes off your dress.

As everyone was filing out, you turned to me and said, "Have a good weekend."

"You too," I said.

I watched you walk away. Your step, like your body, was lithe.

Waiting for my sandwich, I saw you disappear into the dining room. This time, I followed you.

I saw you sitting alone at a table next to a window. In the sunlight, you looked older and even lovelier.

You smiled as I approached your table.

"Would you like some company?" I asked.

"I'd love some," you said.

The Discord in Our Soul

Carlos Garcia pushed open the door. The small office was empty and dark. As he closed the door behind him, he saw three Secret Service men, looking stoic, take up positions as sentries outside in the hallway.

For a moment, he thought about flipping on the light. But the near darkness suited his mood. A frosted glass panel in the door let in just enough light for him to make out a desk. He stepped over to it. He felt for the edge of the desktop and, pushing down on it with the palm of his right hand, lowered himself down on one knee, as if he were genuflecting. Then he knelt down completely.

Folding his hands and bowing his head, he closed his eyes. He had come there to pray. But he couldn't pray. His heart was beating too fast, and his mind was reeling from the awful flurry of events of the past hour.

Just an hour ago, he had been in the Oval Office upstairs, enjoying the first meeting of his presidency. It was with the leaders of the Boy Scouts along with a few scouts themselves and their parents. It was an opportunity for Garcia to express his genuine appreciation to an organization which had helped shape his young life—and to start his presidency on an earnest note.

But no sooner had that meeting begun than two Secret Service men burst into the room.

"Mr. President," one of them said loudly, "We must ask you to come with us to the Situation Room immediately."

Garcia looked annoyed and began to apologize to his guests.

"Now, sir!" the other Secret Service man exclaimed, stepping toward the President.

"Okay," Garcia said, getting up and following the two men to the door.

On his way out, he glanced back at his guests, who sat there, looking bewildered and afraid.

In the Situation Room, he learned that, about 10 minutes earlier, North Korea had fired eight nuclear missiles at the United States.

Without hesitation, the President ordered his Secretary of Defense, Tom Adams, to use all conventional weapons necessary to shoot them down. Less than 10 minutes later, radar confirmed that the countermeasures were successful.

All eight missiles were destroyed over the oceans. Some were taken out by missiles fired by fighter jets and drones as the nukes rose toward the atmosphere. Most were destroyed by interceptor rockets upon re-entry.

After a brief celebration, the President's advisors put forward their recommendations for a more complete response. They fell into three camps.

First were the doves, led by Garcia's Secretary of State, Rachel Phillips.

"The international community will be with us, Mr. President," she said. "No one can abide such egregious action. We can propose international sanctions through the UN and mandatory inspections of all nuclear facilities in North Korea. In this way, we can prevent any further threat, and our restraint will enhance our credibility on the world stage. It will be seen as a sign of strength."

The second group was led by Garcia's National Security Advisor, Gordon Matthews.

"Mr. President, we don't know if North Korea has used its entire stockpile of weapons. We can't take a chance. We must destroy all its military bases as well as any suspected nuclear sites. Doing so is a proportional response and the only way we'll know we are safe."

The third group was led by Tom Adams.

"Mr. President, this was an act of war. It demands more than a proportional response. We need to send a message that cannot be misunderstood—that this will never happen again. I agree we should take out the military bases and nuclear sites. But I also recommend targeted bombing of the capital buildings in Pyongyang as well as Kim Jong Un's residences. No one will begrudge us such action, Mr. President. Everyone knows that those eight nuclear missiles, had they reached their targets, would have killed millions of our people."

"How many lives would be lost?" Garcia asked.

"Hundreds of thousands," Adams said. "Maybe a million."

The President sat in silence.

"Any other recommendations?" he asked.

He looked around the table. No one said a word. Then Adams said, "Mr. President, you must decide soon."

"How much time do I have, Tom?"

"You need to decide now, sir."

"Tom," said Garcia, sounding weary, "you're asking me to make a decision that could cost a million lives. How much time do I have?"

"Mr. President. With respect, we still don't know if more missiles will be fired. Every minute we fail to act is a minute we leave ourselves in jeopardy."

The President removed his glasses and looked directly at Adams.

"How much time, Tom?"

"Fifteen minutes."

"All right," said Garcia, standing up. "I'll be back in 10 minutes."

"Where are you going, Mr. President?" asked Secretary Phillips.

"Just down the hall," said Garcia, heading for the door. "I need a moment alone."

#

Eighteen months earlier, the whole country had been in a rancorous mood, and the primaries and presidential debates only made things worse.

Everybody knew the national conventions would be a circus that summer. Had he not been a delegate to the GOP convention, Carlos Garcia, the popular governor of New Mexico, wouldn't have attended.

In politics, Garcia was an anomaly. He was soft-spoken and easy-going, the son of Mexican immigrants, a former seminarian. People called him a Boy Scout because he refused to engage in behavior he considered disrespectful. But in his own quiet way, he managed to bring people together and get things done.

Garcia wanted to skip the convention. He knew it would be wild, but he went because he was pledged to go.

On the first day, the presumptive nominee's support began to splinter. On the second, delegates began to occupy different spots in the hall, rallying around their respective candidates. As they began to shout and even hurl objects at one another, the convention floor took on the look of a battlefield.

On the third day, riots broke out in the streets. Party leaders considered calling the whole thing off and reconvening later. But they concluded that doing so would only make matters worse, so they pressed on.

On the fourth day, at last, names began to be placed in nomination, but there was no consensus — only more bitter disagreement.

On the fifth day, the presumed nominee stormed out, declaring the whole thing a sham and announcing he might run as an independent candidate.

That evening, Jose Rivas, Garcia's longtime friend and fellow delegate from New Mexico, approached the governor. He told him his state's delegation wanted to place his name in nomination.

"You must be kidding," Garcia said.

"Carlos," said Rivas. "Look around you. You might be our only hope."

"I wouldn't stand a chance, Jose."

"We need you, Carlos. The country needs you."

Garcia was not without ambition, but he had never desired any office beyond governor of his state. Not that he hadn't thought about the presidency. He simply couldn't see himself in that role.

"I'm a pacifist," he once said to his wife. "How could I ever be Commander in Chief?"

But Garcia was also a patriot, and it broke his heart to see his country so divided. Now, he, a man who had a special talent for bringing people together, was being asked to do that on a grander scale than he had ever imagined.

"I'll think about it overnight," he told his friend Jose.

Garcia went to his hotel that night thinking he would say no in the morning. As he sat in a lumpy armchair in the corner of his room, he remembered how he had felt, as a boy, when he started thinking about becoming a priest. It wasn't the idea of being a priest that was so intriguing. It was the notion of being called. Now, he was experiencing that feeling again.

"Go ahead," he told Jose the next morning.

That afternoon, on the ninth ballot, Garcia's name was placed in nomination.

On the seventh day and the twelfth ballot, a majority of delegates voted for Garcia, and he became the party's nominee.

It was a desperation move. Party leaders and delegates alike knew that, but in all the chaos that year, they also knew no one else of any stature could be nominated. Garcia might be bland, but at least he wasn't polarizing.

A week later, the Democrats nominated their frontrunner, but only after their own melee. Heated arguments about the party platform boiled over into fistfights. Chairs flew. Outside, police had to use pepper spray to control the crowd. Commentators began comparing it to the Democratic national convention in 1968. Dozens were injured, some seriously, before the whole thing was brought to an early end.

After the convention, things got worse. Every day, a demonstration. Every night, a riot. Twenty-thousand Americans moved to Toronto.

During the general election campaign, Garcia's opponent attacked him daily, but he didn't take the bait. Instead, he treated her with respect. As a result, many voters gave him a second look. People began to rally around Garcia. *Time* magazine called him "the un-candidate." That November, he won decisively.

However, if the majority of voters wanted Garcia as President, he himself had misgivings. He had never envisioned himself as President. Deep down, he wondered if he was the right man for the job.

#

Now, he had a decision to make. Kneeling in the near darkness made him think back to morning prayers when he was in the seminary. They always started promptly at 5:30, just before the sun rose. The only light in the chapel came from two candles at the sides of the altar.

Sermons during morning prayers were rare. In fact, Garcia could remember only one.

It was one he would never forget. That morning, Father Aldric, one of the older priests, chose to focus on one of the Beatitudes.

"Blessed are the peacemakers for they shall be called sons of God."

Father Aldric explained why this idea was central not only in the teachings of Jesus but also in the life of St. Francis of Assisi.

He remembered Father Aldric raising his eyes, stretching out his arms and singing, "Lord, make me an instrument of thy peace."

This message and the image of Father Aldric, a man who had devoted his life to God, were burned into Garcia's young mind. They were seeds planted in his soul.

Ultimately, he decided to leave the seminary. Not because he no longer felt his life had a higher purpose. In fact, before he left,

Garcia made a private vow that he would always be a man of peace. He was simply not sure he was selfless enough to be a priest.

Garcia heard a low, inaudible voice in the hallway. It reminded him of the awful decision that lay before him.

He thought about the oath of office he had taken less than a day ago.

"I do solemnly swear that I will faithfully execute the Office of the President of the United States ... So help me God."

For Garcia, it was a singular moment, though not an entirely new experience. It was the seventh time he had taken an oath of office. The first had been as a new councilman in Albuquerque, nearly 30 years earlier.

The idea of supporting the Constitution had not just become a part of his creed. It had become the focus of his life. He had devoted his career to upholding the Constitution.

Now, he must choose. He must, in effect, decide which of his callings was more important—his oath or his vow.

At that moment, he felt as though he were living in two dimensions — one present, knowing there could be more missiles yet to be launched; the other future, knowing that history will define his presidency by the decision he alone must make in the coming minutes.

His conscience, his responsibility, his legacy. They were all compressed into that crucible moment.

Someone rapped at the door.

"Mr. President, it's time."

Tears welled in Garcia's eyes. His whole body trembled. He imagined Jesus on his knees in the garden, knowing what had to happen, yet asking his father to let the cup pass.

In agony, Garcia asked God to quiet the discord in his soul. Then his choice became clear, and he got up.

Beauty Mark

Claire Wilson had never been so happy. Two days ago, she had graduated from high school. Yesterday, she had signed a contract with a top modeling agency in New York City. She would start in two weeks. She was all set to take a train with her parents to New York that weekend to find a place to live. Her lifelong dream of becoming a model was about to come true.

Now, as she was stepping out of the shower, Claire slipped on the wet tile floor. She fell so fast that she had no time to extend her hands to grab onto anything. The right side of her face hit the laminated corner of the sink, tearing a deep gash from her jawline to her hairline. The impact knocked her sideways and back against the bathroom wall.

From the kitchen, her mother heard the thud, and then she heard Claire cry out. She rushed in and found her daughter lying naked on the floor, with blood streaming from her head and covering her face.

#

Claire had been such a beautiful baby — curly blond hair, powder blue eyes, charming dimples. She'd looked like she belonged on a package of Pampers.

As she grew older, Claire grew even lovelier. In grade school, all the girls wanted to look like her. In high school, all the boys wanted to be with her. On the street or in stores, passersby would do a double take. Some would even stop and stare.

Claire enjoyed being the center of attention. It made her feel special. She loved hearing people say, "You should be a model." As a girl, she had been drawn to the glamorous women in the ads in her mother's magazines. She dreamed of being on a magazine cover one day.

When Claire was a teenager, her mother arranged for her to be professionally photographed. Her mom sent her photos to the top modeling agencies in New York. By the time she graduated from high school, Claire had her pick of agencies. They'd been jockeying for her.

The day after she graduated, Claire chose the largest agency. She was impressed by their claim that their models had appeared on more fashion magazine covers than those from all the other top agencies combined.

They'd offered Claire a generous contract. She had just signed it and come home from mailing it at the post office when she decided to take a shower.

#

Claire's injury required more than 100 stitches. The emergency room surgeon closed the gaping wound, but the damage to her face was extensive. It would take a series of operations to advance the healing process.

The cost of the first two of those surgeries, to reconnect muscle and nerves, would be covered by the talent agency's medical insurance. After that, the surgeries would be considered cosmetic, and they weren't covered by the agency's policy. Hopeful that Claire might still have a shot at modeling, her parents dipped into their savings to cover the costs.

During the next four months, Claire underwent several more procedures. Fortunately, her doctors were successful in repairing much of the damage to her face, and only a faint scar remained. Unfortunately, it was slightly raised and noticeable, even with makeup. After reviewing new photos of Claire's face, the talent agency chose to exercise an escape clause in her contract.

The agency was merely confirming what Claire had known from the moment her head hit that sink, that her career in modeling — her dream — was over.

#

Yet Claire did not accept her fate easily.

"Why has this happened to me?" she sobbed to her mother.

"Claire, honey, I don't know. I'm so sorry."

"The only thing I've ever wanted to be was a model."

"I know, honey."

"Well, what I am supposed to do now?"

"Claire, you're so talented. You have a lot of other options."

"Like what, mom?"

"Well, what are your other interests?"

"Mom! I have no other interests! I just wanted to be a model. And now that's never going to happen!"

Claire pounded her fists on the arms of the recliner she was sitting in and lurched forward, slamming the footrest into the base of the chair. She sprung to her feet and stomped across the family room and into the kitchen.

Her mother heard car keys scrape against a wooden board on the wall next to the door to the garage.

"Where you are going, honey?"

"Out!" Claire screamed, slamming the door behind her.

She got in her mom's car, pulled out of the driveway and sped down the street. She drove through the streets of her small town, the only place she'd ever lived. She drove past her grade school, where she'd been crowned the May Queen, and her high school, where she'd been crowned Homecoming queen. These were among the happiest moments of her life. She wondered if she could ever be happy again.

Claire flew into tantrums all that summer. Her parents tried to console her, telling her that her face kept looking so much better, that she was still beautiful. It was true, but it was not what Claire wanted to hear. She wanted someone to tell her she should be a model again, but she knew she never would.

The attention she had always enjoyed, even craved, she now avoided. She hated bumping into people she knew. That summer, she ran into Mrs. Adkins, a neighbor, in the grocery store.

"Claire!" she called, spotting her in the cereal aisle. "How are you?"

Claire could feel the woman's eyes on her face.

"Good, Mrs. Adkins. I'm good."

"I was so sorry to hear about your accident."

"Thank you."

"But it looks like your face is healing very nicely."

"Thank you."

Claire knew Mrs. Adkins was lying. She knew her face would never be flawless again.

#

That fall, as her friends left for college, Claire fell into a pattern of driving her mother's car, aimlessly, through the streets.

She drove past her favorite stores, friends' houses, the photograph studio where she'd posed for modeling agency shots, her schools, her church. These places made up the only world she had ever known.

But now she began to long for something more. One day, she drove to the edge of town and kept driving. She came to a small college. She hadn't been there. She drove slowly through the tree-lined streets, watching students stroll along the sidewalks.

A large, red-brick building with a portico supported by white columns caught her eye. It was magnificent. She stopped and parked her car.

She got out and walked up to the building. Standing close, she could see that some of the bricks were cracked, some of the mortar was broken and some of the paint was chipped. Claire realized that had she seen these imperfections from the street, she would have thought the building no less beautiful.

She started walking toward the center of campus. Students passing by smiled and said hello. She felt welcome there. She began to feel like herself again.

She found the admissions office, went inside and applied for enrollment in the spring.

#

In her sophomore year, Claire declared psychology as her major. She ended up with both a master's degree and a doctorate in psychology. Her dissertation was on "redefining beauty."

"We all tend to see ourselves as imperfect," she wrote. "'If only I could fix this one thing,' we say to ourselves. But what we first see as a flaw we come to realize is our beauty mark. It allows us to see our real beauty, our truest beauty, in a way we might otherwise never know."

Claire started giving talks to high school girls on this theme, sharing her own journey. *Glamour* magazine heard about her talks. They interviewed her, did a feature story on her and put her on the cover.

Delivered

December 22, 10:39 a.m.

She knew better, but having just finished her second cup of coffee, she had to go to the bathroom, and Jake seemed so content, playing with his cars and trucks on the patio. Besides, she would be only a minute or two.

She was sitting on the toilet when she heard Alfie, their toy poodle, barking, high-pitched and non-stop. She hurried to finish and headed for the back door. As soon as she opened it, she spotted Alfie jumping up and down near the back corner of the wire-meshed, split-rail fence, which rimmed their back yard. He was barking furiously in the direction of the shallow woods just beyond the fence.

Jake was not on the patio. She looked around. He was nowhere in sight. She called his name, but there was no answer. She sprinted to his playhouse in the middle of the yard and looked inside. He wasn't there. She darted around the yard, searching behind every tree and bush. Sometimes, he liked to play hide and seek there. But not today.

"Jake!" she called. "Jake!"

She ran around the house and into the woods. She was having a hard time catching her breath. She could hear her heart beating hard and fast in her ears. She felt dizzy. She began screaming, "Jake! Jake! Jake!"

Then she thought of how she had left him, not 10 minutes earlier, and felt sick. She fell to her knees and threw up in the grass.

#

She went inside and called her next-door neighbors, but neither had seen her little boy. *What should she do now? Call her husband at work? The police? Continue to search on her own?*

She looked out into the back yard through the kitchen window. Jake was out there somewhere. She had no idea where, but she knew she needed help. She picked up her phone and dialed 911.

"Hello, my name is Kate Foster. I live at 242 Wabash Court in Fairfax. My little boy, Jake, is missing. He was playing on our patio. I went inside for just a few minutes, and when I came back, he was gone. He's not even two, and we have a fenced-in back yard, so he couldn't have run away. I think somebody—she swallowed, almost choking on the word—kidnapped him."

"Okay, ma'am. I'm going to ask you a few questions."

"Okay."

"When did you last see your son?"

"About 15 minutes ago."

"What was he wearing?

"Jeans. He's wearing blue jeans."

"What else?"

"A red wool cap, a blue coat and light brown shoes."

"And you say he's about two?"

"Yes, he'll turn two on Christmas."

"And his name is Jake?"

"Yes."

"Okay, ma'am. I'll send a police officer over right away. I'll also issue an alert to all our officers in the area to keep watch for Jake. Someone should be at your house within 10 minutes. So please stay there."

"I will. Thank you."

Kate hung up. She had been pacing around the kitchen. Suddenly, her knees felt weak, and she collapsed on a chair at the kitchen table.

It was a small, square table. To her left sat a blue, plastic booster seat. Jake's chair. As soon as she saw it, she began sobbing.

Then she thought of her husband, Joe. She needed to call him before the police arrived. She needed to compose herself. So she got up, grabbed a tissue, blew her nose and wiped her eyes, then made the toughest phone call of her life.

#

Kate was on the patio with Officer Garrett, going over what happened, when Joe got home. He opened the back door, and she ran to him. She threw her arms around him and started crying again.

"Joe, I'm so sorry," she sobbed. "I left him for only a minute. But I shouldn't have done it. I shouldn't have done it. Oh, Joe! I'm so sorry!"

"It's okay, Kate. You didn't do anything wrong. We'll find Jake. It will be okay."

She knew that he couldn't possibly know this. But she took comfort in his words and felt grateful he was there and she could hold him.

Officer Garrett introduced himself.

"Your wife was just telling me that when she came back out of the house this morning, your dog was barking in the back corner of your yard, near the fence."

"Do you think that's where the kidnapper got away?" Joe asked.

"I have a strong suspicion it was. How deep are those woods, sir?"

"Not deep at all."

"There are houses on the other side," Kate said.

"Another subdivision?"

"Yes," Joe said.

"I'm going to call in and get a team out here to canvas the woods while there's still plenty of light. They'll also want to question the neighbors and the people living on the other side of the woods. Let me make that call now, then we can wrap up your report."

"Okay," they said.

Officer Garrett walked around the back yard, talking into his Bluetooth headset. Kate and Joe held each other on the patio. Kate could not stop crying.

"They're sending a team over right away," said Officer Garrett, stepping back onto the patio. "If it's okay with you, I'll stay until they get here."

"Yes, of course," Joe said.

Kate and Joe were holding hands. Kate looked down. She was standing in the middle of Jake's toys, in the place she had last seen him, the place she had left him. She turned away, buried her head in Joe's chest and began crying even harder.

"I know how upsetting this is," the officer said. "Fortunately, our track record of finding missing children is very good."

"Really?" Kate asked, unburying her head.

"Well, there are no guarantees, of course. But we'll certainly do our best."

"Thank you, officer," Joe said. "So what are our next steps?"

Kate was so glad Joe was there. She would never have thought to ask such a thing, not at a time like this. She was grateful for his cool head. She sometimes gave him a hard time for being so logical, but not now.

Officer Garrett said his team would be searching the woods and interviewing neighbors for several hours. He explained the "dragnet" system his department used, working with other law enforcement authorities in the area and even the FBI. They maintained a hotline for tips and would be issuing a news release. He said they would need a photo of Jake for that.

"A news release?" Joe asked.

"Yes, we want to raise awareness and call on the community to help us."

He sensed some hesitation.

"Are you okay with a news release?"

"I guess so," Joe said slowly. "It's just that I never imagined that kind of exposure."

"I know it feels strange. But it can help."

"Yes, we're okay with a news release," Kate said. "Where should I send the photo?"

"Email it to me," the officer said, handing Kate his card. "In fact, if you have any questions, any time, I want you to call me. And if we get any leads or have any new information, I'll call you."

"Thank you," she said, stuffing his card into her pocket. Just then, the doorbell rang, and Alfie started barking.

"I think our team is here," the officer said.

#

They were in the woods for only a few minutes when one of the men in the search party emerged with a red wool hat.

"That's Jake's hat!" Kate cried. "What does this mean?"

"Well, it means we have our first lead," Officer Garrett said. "We have a trail. Now we need to follow it."

There were no other clues in the woods. But one of the neighbors in the subdivision on the other side said she saw a young man getting into a car parked on her street with a small child just before eleven that morning.

She didn't get a good look at him, and she could only describe the car as "small, gray and beat-up." But it was another clue and, based on it, Officer Garrett filed the case as a kidnapping.

#

That day, there were no new leads. By mid-afternoon, the team began to pack up. Officer Garrett, who had stayed the whole time, was the last to leave.

"Don't lose hope," he said. "We will get through this."

"Thank you, officer," Joe said.

"Yes, thank you," Kate added, "for all you're doing to find our son."

#

Kate and Joe went into the kitchen and sat down at the table. Their house felt so empty. It felt so strange not to have Jake there.

They talked about what they should do and decided, at least for the moment, to stay put. And so they sat at the kitchen table with their laptops and cell phones in front of them. Kate remembered to email a photo of Jake to Officer Garrett.

Then they started calling family members and friends. They took turns calling, so that one of their phones was always free, just in case the police were trying to get through.

About an hour later, they saw the first news story, online. When Kate saw the picture of Jake, she buried her face in her hands and started crying so hard that she couldn't speak.

Joe got up and put his arm around her. "Kate, why don't you lie down for a minute?"

He helped her to the sofa in the family room. He put a pillow under her head as she lay down and kissed her on the forehead. Then his cell phone rang. He hurried back to the kitchen to answer it.

It was a reporter for a local TV station. He said he was covering the story and wanted to know if Joe or Kate would be open to an on-camera interview.

"No," Joe said, looking at his wife on the sofa. "We're not ready for that right now."

"I understand," the reporter said. "If you change your mind, just give me a call."

"Thanks. I will."

Jake's kidnapping was the lead story on the 6:00 news. As soon as it aired, Kate and Joe began getting email messages and phone calls from dozens of people who wanted to express their support and offer their help. The sentiment was wonderful, but the volume was overwhelming.

By 9:00, the phone calls began to wane, but the email kept flowing. Neither Joe nor Kate could keep up with it.

They hadn't heard from Officer Garrett.

"Do you think it's too late to call him?" Kate asked.

"No. He said to call any time. Do you want me to do it?"

"Would you?"

"Sure. What's his number?"

Kate reached into her pocket and slipped his card across the table.

Officer Garrett was at home. He apologized for not reaching out, even though there were no new tips or leads to report.

"I'll call you in the morning, regardless," he said.

"Okay," Joe said. "We'd appreciate that. Good night."

Joe and Kate continued responding to email messages until just before midnight. They were utterly exhausted.

"I think we should try to get some sleep," Joe said.

"I can't go to bed without Jake here."

"Kate, I know it's hard. But we've got to get some rest or else we'll be no good to anybody."

She let out a long, low, sorrowful whine. Joe got up to console her. She put her arms around his neck, and he held her close.

"I'm sorry, Joe," she sobbed.

"Kate, it's okay," he said. He reached his left arm around her back, slipped his right arm under her legs and picked her up. He carried her slowly across the kitchen, then up the stairs to their bedroom. He laid her down gently on their bed, then grabbed a blanket and pulled it over both of them.

She was lying on her back. He reached across her, cupping her shoulder in his hand, and kissed her cheek. At last, she had fallen asleep.

#

December 23, 7:14 a.m.

Brandon Ward was a thief. He had stolen things all his life: money, food, clothes, bikes, silverware, tools, furniture, computers, TVs, jewelry, cars. Once, he even stole a chuck roast slow-cooking in a crock pot. But until yesterday, he had never stolen a human being.

Now, he was beginning to regret it.

His plan had seemed so simple. Find a house in an upscale neighborhood, kidnap a kid when no one was looking and demand a hefty ransom.

But as successful as he was at stealing things, Brandon Ward was not very smart. He didn't have to be. Breaking into houses is mainly about patience and speed, not intelligence.

Stealing a child is much different, and Brandon hadn't given any thought to two very important considerations. First, how to pull off a ransom without getting caught. Second, how to care for a two-year-old who isn't potty-trained.

Stealing the boy wasn't hard. He had been watching a row of houses from the woods bordering their back yards for a week. He figured out when their mothers brought them outside to play. With the winter weather so mild, kids were out nearly every day. He knew it was only a matter of time before some mother left her child out there for a minute or two. And that was all the time he needed to grab the kid and run through the shallow woods to his car.

He had been watching Jake on the patio and saw Kate go inside. No sooner had she shut the door than he jumped over the fence, nimble and quiet as a cat. In less than a minute, he had grabbed Jake and climbed back over the fence. He was concerned that the boy might call out, but he didn't. The dog was on his heels, though. He hated dogs.

Brandon was almost through the woods when he heard a woman behind him calling "Jake!" He could feel the boy turn his head toward the sound of his mother's voice, but still he did not call out. Instead, he whimpered, "Mommy."

By then, Brandon had made it through the woods. He ran through the unfenced yard on the other side, straight to his car, which he had parked on the street. He opened the driver's side door, dumped the boy into the passenger's seat, jumped in and drove away. He checked his rear view mirror on his way out of the subdivision but saw no one.

In a few minutes, he was on the highway, heading for his apartment 20 miles away, on the edge of downtown. About five minutes into drive, he began thinking about the shortcomings of his plan, or lack thereof.

That's when the boy began crying and Brandon first thought about giving him something to eat and realized he had nothing in his place that a two year old might like. He thought about driving through McDonald's but didn't want to risk being seen. So he kept driving, even as the boy kept crying.

"It's okay," he kept saying, hoping to quiet the boy. But he only got louder. By the time they were near Brandon's apartment, he was screaming. He certainly couldn't bring him inside this way.

So he decided to keep driving. He drove five miles or so past his exit until he came to a mom-and-pop store where he had never been and, he hoped, would not be recognized.

But what should he do with the kid? He couldn't bring him inside, not crying like this. So he decided to park on the side of the store, out of sight, and lock the doors, with the boy buckled in his seat belt. There was no guarantee, of course, that someone wouldn't hear him and call the cops. But it was a risk he was going to have to take.

He ducked into the store, grabbed one of the small shopping carts lined up inside the door and dashed up and down the aisles, throwing an assortment of items into the cart: SpaghettiOs, Cheerios, apple juice, milk, bread, peanut butter, jelly, bologna, chocolate chip cookies, candy bars — and, of course, a package of diapers. He even found a sippy cup.

He checked out, grabbed the bags of groceries and hurried to his car. He expected the boy would still be screaming. Instead, he was just sitting there, quietly sobbing.

Brandon opened the back door and threw the bags onto the back seat. He pulled out the package of cookies, tore it open and took one out.

"Here you go," he said to the boy, handing him the cookie as he got in the car.

The boy immediately stopped crying, grabbed the cookie with both hands and took a big bite. Brandon was learning.

He parked the car behind his apartment building. He snagged all the plastic grocery bags in his right hand, fished the boy out of the car with his left, bumped the car doors closed with his butt and slowly made his way up the stairs to his second-floor apartment, carefully balancing the boy and the bags of groceries. Stealing TVs was a lot easier.

Once inside, the boy started crying again. Brandon took off his coat, gave him another cookie and sat him down on the couch. Sure enough, he stopped crying again. *I should have bought more cookies*, he thought.

The apartment was tiny. It consisted of a living room, a kitchen, a bedroom and a bathroom. The living room and kitchen were essentially one room. Brandon took off his coat and hat and began unpacking the groceries in the kitchen. The boy could see him from the couch.

"Milk!" he yelled, as Brandon pulled a gallon of milk out of one of the plastic bags.

"You want some milk?"

"Milk!"

"Okay," Brandon said. He grabbed the sippy cup, filled it with milk, snapped the lid on tight and handed it to the boy. He grabbed it and drank it down thirstily.

Then Brandon put the groceries away. Seeing the diapers reminded him the boy was ready, probably past ready, for a change. He tore open the package, pulled out a diaper and walked over to the couch. He stood there, frozen, for a moment. He had never changed a diaper, and he wasn't sure exactly where to begin.

But when the boy saw the diaper, he slid off the couch and lay down on his back on the floor. Brandon was amazed — and happy to follow the boy's lead. He pulled down his pants and proceeded to change one very wet and heavy diaper.

Then the boy clambered back up onto the couch and continued drinking his milk. After a few more gulps, he dropped the sippy cup onto the cushion. A little milk dribbled out of the spout. Brandon grabbed the cup, then went into the kitchen for a paper towel to sop up the milk. When he returned, the boy was rubbing his eyes. He looked tired.

"Do you need a nap?" Brandon asked.

"Nap," the boy mumbled.

Holy crap, Brandon thought. *I really should have thought this through.*

For a moment, he considered laying the boy down on the couch. But he was probably going to watch TV and thought that might keep him awake. So he carried him into his bedroom, laid him down on his bed and covered him with a blanket.

"Night, night," the boy said.

Brandon closed the blinds. By the time he turned around, the boy had fallen asleep.

Brandon walked back into the living room but kept the bedroom door open. He grabbed the remote and turned on the TV.

"Police found the boy's hat in a nearby woods," the news anchor was reporting. "They believe the kidnapper escaped with the boy through the woods, then took off with him in a gray, compact car. The police are asking anyone who has seen this boy to contact them. Here is that hotline number again."

On the screen was a photo of the boy and his name, Jake Foster, the boy he had taken this morning, the little boy now asleep on his bed.

Brandon changed the channel. Same story. He switched channels. Same story there too. *Christmas Kidnapping.* It was headline news.

Good Lord, he thought. He suspected there would be some publicity, but nothing like this.

He turned off the TV and looked around the room. His place was so small. That had never bothered him before. Now that he knew people were on the lookout for the boy, and maybe him too, his little apartment began to feel like a prison.

The irony was that he had hoped this would be his big break. Between the money he made pawning and working odd jobs, he was doing okay financially. He had grown weary of living in the shadows, of always feeling he had to watch his back.

He had lived this way for three years, since he was 16. That's when he decided he could no longer take his mother's abuse and left home. He took a bus to a city nearly 300 miles away and started a new life.

At first, it seemed cool, even a bit glamorous. Soon he realized that, in any city, when you depend on pawnbrokers for your income, they get to know you, and when you're always just one step ahead of the police, it's never a good thing to become well-known by pawnbrokers.

So he had to keep moving. In three years, he had lived in three different cities. And he was tired of moving. He was tired of being on the run. He had begun to imagine a fresh start. He imagined moving far away, changing his name, getting a real job, making friends.

He imagined these things, but his "plan" for just how he would make his big break was sorely lacking. In his mind, he simply envisioned snatching a kid, demanding a ransom, grabbing the money and skipping town. It worked that way on TV. But as he finally began to think it through, he realized there was no way he could pull it off without getting caught.

He needed a new plan, a real plan, a plan that would deliver him from the dark and lonely place that had become his life.

#

December 24, 6:37 a.m.

Kate Foster felt like a zombie. She had been awake for most of the past 48 hours, unable to sleep as the police searched in vain for her missing son.

But Jake's absence was not the only thing keeping her awake. It was not the only thing tormenting her.

Five years earlier, Kate had married Joe. They were very much in love, but Kate was in love with another man too.

His name was Matt. Kate was dating him when she met Joe. And unknown to Joe, she kept seeing Matt when she and Joe got engaged and even after they were married.

Kate knew it was wrong, and both she and Matt tried to break it off. They would go weeks without seeing each other, but they always managed to find their way back together.

Kate had been intimate with Matt not long before she became pregnant with Jake. But she had been with Joe so much longer that she put any thought of this not being his child out of her mind.

Until the baby was born. Jake was blond-haired and blue-eyed, just like Matt. In fact, he looked nothing like Joe. But Joe fell in love with the boy, and if he ever suspected anything, he never let on.

Matt had dropped out of her life when he heard that she was pregnant. He never made another attempt to reach her, and she never saw him again. He may have suspected that he was Jake's biological father and wanted to be far away in case there was trouble.

Any inclination to reach out to Matt dissipated the moment Jake was born because, from that moment on, Joe was the most loving father any mother or child could ever hope for. He got up with Kate for breastfeeding during the night. He helped give Jake his first bath. He crawled on the floor with him as he was learning to crawl. He fed him, took him on walks, played with him for hours. He was the perfect father.

All of which Kate loved, of course, but all of which served to make her feel even worse for what she had done and for keeping it from Joe — the best man she had ever known and the man she now loved with all her heart.

Losing Jake was now tearing her apart, but it was tearing Joe apart too. He too could hardly sleep. He too paced the floor not knowing what to do. But unlike Matt, Joe was now there for Kate, holding her, comforting her, telling her it would be okay.

She had considered telling her husband the truth a thousand times but could never bring herself to do it. It was her great secret and her great sin. It weighed on her like an anchor she had to drag unseen through her daily life, an anchor that seemed to get heavier and more unbearable by the day. She knew how to unburden herself—by divulging the truth. But that was the one thing she somehow could not find a way to do.

Now, though, as she awoke from her fragmentary slumber, looking over at Joe asleep with his clothes on and his arm draped over her waist, she decided that when they had found Jake, she would tell him everything.

#

Just before noon, Joe's phone rang. It was a number he didn't recognize, but he answered it.

"Hello?"

"Mr. Foster? This is Steve Atkins, Channel 12 news. We spoke by phone a couple of days ago."

"Oh, yes."

"I'm sorry to see your son is still missing."

"Thank you. Is there something I can do for you?"

"Actually, Mr. Foster, I was wondering if there is something I can do for you."

"What do you mean?"

"I know when we spoke a couple of days ago, you were not inclined to do an interview. But I was hoping you might reconsider."

"Why would I do that?"

"Well, I've noticed that even though there's been a fair amount of media coverage of your son's kidnapping, you or your wife have not done any interviews."

"And?"

"I think that would make this story even more compelling. An on-air appeal to the kidnapper by you or your wife could really help."

"You think that might actually work?"

"There are no guarantees, of course. But I've seen it work before."

Joe paused. "When would we do this?"

"I could come to your house any time."

"Let me call you right back."

"Okay."

"Who was that?" Kate asked.

"It was a reporter for Channel 12 news. He wants to interview one of us. He claims an appeal by one of us to the kidnapper on TV might work."

"What do you think?" Kate asked.

"I think he's just trying to bump his ratings."

"But do you think it might work?"

"I think it's a long shot."

"Joe, it's our son. I think it's worth taking a long shot."

He was surprised. "Are you willing to do an on-camera interview?" he asked.

"Yes."

"Are you sure?"

"Joe, I hate the idea. But I'll do it. I'll do it if it will help us find Jake."

Joe called the reporter back.

"My wife, Kate, will do the interview. But I want you to handle it personally. Can you be here at three?"

#

Brandon finished spreading the jelly, stuck the slices of bread together and cut the sandwich into small squares. Then he put it on a plate and brought it into the living room, where Jake was sitting on the couch, sipping his milk. Cheerios were scattered all around him.

"Here you go, big guy."

The boy's eyes lit up when he saw the sandwich.

"Sammich!" he called out, reaching for the plate. Brandon set it down on his lap. The boy tossed aside his sippy cup, grabbed a piece of the sandwich and stuffed it into his mouth.

This kid never stops eating, Brandon thought.

With the boy digging into his PB&J, Brandon switched the channel from cartoons to the news.

Mother of kidnapped boy speaks out at 6:00 read the words scrolling across the bottom of the screen. Brandon looked at the clock. It was a few minutes before six.

"Stay right here," he said as he stepped into the kitchen and grabbed a can of beer. He got back just as the newscast was starting.

"Good evening," the anchor said. "I'm Sarah Daniels. Over the past two days, we've been reporting on the disappearance of a two-year-old Fairfax boy named Jake Foster in what is being called 'the Christmas kidnapping.' Until now, his parents have not spoken out. This evening, Jake's mother, Kate, breaks her silence in an exclusive interview with Channel 12's Steve Atkins."

An image of the patio from which he had taken the boy flashed up on the screen.

"It was here, on the patio of this home in Fairfax, just after 10:30 on Tuesday morning, that Kate Foster last saw her son, Jake," the reporter intoned.

As he spoke, the images changed from the patio to the backyard, the woods and the street where Brandon had driven away with the boy.

"Jake's mother, Kate, agreed to an interview here in her home because she says wants to speak directly to whoever has taken her little boy."

Brandon had seen her only from a distance, from the woods. Now her face filled the screen.

"Mommy!" the boy laughed, pointing to the TV.

"Yeah," Brandon said, patting the boy's knee. "Mommy."

Kate was sitting on her living room sofa. As she spoke, she looked into the camera.

"I don't know who you are or why you've taken my son. But I know that, to do such a thing, you must be broken. I know something about brokenness because I'm broken too."

She cleared her throat, then went on.

"Keeping Jake won't help you. But releasing him can begin to heal your brokenness and mine too. Give him back as a Christmas gift, not just for my sake, but for yours because, by giving him back, you will be forgiven. I will forgive you, and I know that God will forgive you too."

Brandon looked down at the boy. His face was covered with peanut butter and jelly.

Broken. Yeah, Brandon thought. Kate was right about that. He had felt broken for a long time. He knew she was right about giving Jake back too.

How could he do that without getting caught? Every cop in the city was looking for this kid.

Brandon sat back on the couch, took a swig of beer and, for a change, thought deeply about his options.

#

December 24, 10:30 p.m.

As soon as he grabbed the handle of the large wooden door and began to pull, he felt the door being gently pushed opened.

"Merry Christmas," said a man in a suit and tie on the other side. "Welcome to St. Anthony's."

"Merry Christmas," said Brandon, stepping inside with the boy in his arms.

"We're almost full. But there are still a few seats in the back."

"Thank you."

The church was dark, lit only by the glow of dozens of candles around the perimeter. The air smelled like candle wax.

A woman sitting alone at the end of the last pew turned and saw him standing there, holding the boy.

"Sit here," she whispered, motioning to him. "I can scoot down."

"Thank you."

He sat Jake down next to the woman, then squeezed into the space at the end of the pew. The church was warm. He removed the boy's hat, which was actually one of his hats, but kept his own hat on. In the front of the church, a choir, accompanied by a few musicians, sang "O, Holy Night."

Maybe it was the soft music or the flickering candles or the lateness of the hour. But for whatever reason, Jake seemed perfectly content, nestled against Brandon, who put his arm around him. Within a few minutes, the boy was asleep.

"Excuse me," Brandon whispered to the woman next to Jake. "Would you watch him for a minute?"

"Certainly."

Brandon didn't want Jake to fall over, so he laid him down in the pew, placing his hat under his head. The boy slept away.

Brandon got up and made his way to the door. Just to his right, on a marble-topped table against the back wall of the church, sat a nativity scene. He noticed the crib was empty.

He pushed open the heavy oak door and hurried down the worn stone steps to the sidewalk. Halfway down the block was a pay phone. He looked around. No one was watching. He picked up the receiver and dialed 911.

"911, what's your emergency?"

"The Foster kid the police are looking for is in St. Anthony's Church, downtown."

There was a pause.

"Would you repeat that?"

"The Foster kid is at St. Anthony's."

"Who is this?"

He hung up and ran to his car. The police found it two days later in the parking lot of the bus station.

Cut

The lanky man stood at a small table in the corner of the conference room and stirred cream and sugar into his coffee. His hand was shaking.

"Cuts?" he asked.

"Yeah," said an older man, sitting alone at the oblong conference table. He was tense.

"What kind of cuts?"

"Personnel."

"Big?"

"Yeah."

"How big?"

"Paul, I want to wait until the others get here."

"Okay, Bob."

Paul nodded, sat down across from his boss and sipped his coffee. Bob had always been so energetic. Lately, though, he seemed utterly worn out.

Bob had a daunting task. He was the middle man between Lance, the new CEO of the company, who cared only about the balance sheet, and his team, which cared only about developing, making and selling great medical devices. Trying to reconcile these opposing interests, Bob was at loose ends.

The door opened. A petite woman entered the room.

"Good morning, Barb," said Bob. "Help yourself to coffee."

In her mid-50s, Barb was even older than Bob. But she looked about 20 years younger. She was a runner, and she dressed like a fashion model. A mystery to everyone, she had remained single.

"Good morning," Barb said. "What's up?"

"We're going to be announcing some enrollment reductions."

Just then a youthful-looking man in a plaid shirt, navy blue pants and tan shoes walked in.

"Enrollment reductions?" he asked.

"Good morning, Tom," Bob said. "Grab something to drink."

"What kind of enrollment reductions?" Tom asked.

"Let's wait for Julie and Dave," said Bob. "They should be here shortly."

Tom looked at Paul, who was sitting at the conference table, staring blankly into space.

"Okay," said Tom. He walked over to the small table in the corner, squatted down and pulled a Diet Coke out of a small refrigerator underneath.

A minute later, a forty-something woman with short, salt-and-pepper hair walked in. She looked anxious. Ever since battling cancer, she had always seemed on edge.

"What's happening?" she asked.

"Good morning, Julie," Bob said. "Grab some coffee. I've got some organization news to share. We're just waiting for Dave."

"I'm not sure I like the sound of that," said Julie.

A few minutes later, Dave strolled in. He had never been on time for a meeting in his life. But what he lacked in punctuality, he more than made up for in big sales.

He looked around the room. He looked surprised. He was used to seeing this group, the department heads, on Mondays. It was Wednesday.

"What's up?"

"Grab some coffee, Dave," Bob said. "Then we'll get started."

Once they were all seated, Bob began.

"Thank you all for being here, especially on such short notice. I'm afraid I've got some tough news. This Friday, we're going to be announcing a 50 percent reduction in personnel, across the board, all departments."

There were several gasps.

"Did you say 50 percent?"

"Yes."

"You can't be serious."

"I'm afraid I am."

"Why?"

"Lance," said Bob. "Apparently, he's promised the street he's going to shake things up. He wants to tell investors about these cuts and the projected cost savings on the earnings call next Monday."

"He'll shake things up all right," said Tom. "With cuts that deep, we'll go out of business."

In his early 30s, Tom was the only millennial in the group. He had few filters. Bob knew he could always count on Tom to speak his mind, and he encouraged it.

"I share your concern," said Bob.

"What are we going to do?" asked Barb.

"Well," said Bob, "that's why I called you all here. So we can decide how we're going to manage our way through this."

"What's the timeline?"

"We'll make an announcement internally this Friday. It'll go public on Monday. We're all supposed to submit names by next Wednesday. Those people will have four weeks."

"Four weeks?"

"You're kidding!"

"I told you this is going to be tough."

"Tough? It's brutal."

"It's insane!"

"How are we supposed to decide who to let go?"

"Lance is leaving that up to us."

"Well, that's nice of him."

"How in the hell are we supposed to pull this off?" asked Tom.

"To be honest," said Bob, "I'm asking myself the same question."

"What are you saying, Bob?"

"We've all been through downsizings. But nothing like this. We're already lean. Like Tom said, I don't know if we can cut so deep and still run the business."

"Damn straight," said Tom.

Bob looked around the table. These were his people. They were like family. They trusted him. He had never misled them, and he wasn't about to begin now.

"Before we go any farther, let me ask you something."

"Shoot."

"Who here thinks we can run our business with half our people?"

No one raised a hand.

"Nobody?" Bob asked.

"I don't see your hand up, Bob," said Tom.

"Look," Bob said. "All Lance cares about is our stock price. He knows that as soon as we announce these cuts the stock will spike. He's banking on it. So we're going to have to give him something, and it's going to have to be meaningful. Now who wants to put a number on the table?"

Everyone glanced around nervously.

"All right, Bob," said Paul. "Ten percent."

Paul was a functioning alcoholic. Bob had protected him for years, but sometimes Paul really tried his patience.

"Come on, Paul. I'll get thrown out of the room."

"Twenty percent," said Julie. "But no higher."

"I agree with Julie," said Dave. "But if we get rid of 20 percent of our people, we'd better be serious about getting rid of 20 percent of the work."

Three divorce settlements had taught Dave the value of driving a hard bargain.

"Yeah, right," said Tom, rolling his eyes.

"Dave's right," said Barb. "A 20 percent cut in people has to come with a clear commitment to cut 20 percent of the work."

"I hear you," said Bob. "Are we agreed?"

"You mean you'll push back on Lance?"

"I'll push back as hard as I can."

"When?"

"I think I can get a meeting in the morning."

"Good."

"I'll keep you posted. Let's plan to meet back here tomorrow."

"Bob," said Julie. "Hang on."

"What is it?"

"What if Lance says no?"

"What do you mean?"

"I mean, what's our fallback plan?"

"Good question," said Bob. "Options?"

"Well," said Dave. "For starters, I don't think 20 percent is negotiable."

"Do we all agree on that?" Bob asked.

Every head nodded.

"So," Bob said, "what happens if Lance balks at 20 and insists on 50?"

Everyone was fidgeting and looking around.

"Look," Bob said. "You all just agreed we can't run our business with only half our people."

"We were talking about running this business," Tom said.

"What do you mean?" Bob asked.

"I mean that if you sold half the business, maybe then you could make it work."

"Do you think Lance is going to give up half of an empire he just took over, Tom?"

"No."

"But he's willing to part with half of his employees," said Barb.

Bob looked at Barb. He had always seen beyond her beauty. He had long admired her ability to think one step ahead.

"Where are you going with this, Barb?"

"You said it, Bob. Lance is all about the numbers. If he wants to eviscerate his workforce, I have no doubt he'll do it. But he hasn't told us who to let go and who to keep. What if we comply with his ridiculous request and arrange it so that our best employees leave—and we go with them?"

"We go with them?" asked Paul. "Where?"

"We'll form our own company," Barb said. "Smaller. Focused on a few categories, where we can win. We know this business. We know our customers. We know our suppliers. We know the FDA. And we'll have the very best people."

Everyone was looking at Bob. He was not just their boss. He was a father, with two kids in college and a daughter about to get married. He was probably two years from retirement. Starting over at 53 was not part of his plan.

"Is that even an option?" asked Tom.

"Technically, yes," said Bob. "None of us has signed a non-compete clause."

"So what exactly are we proposing?" asked Julie.

"What we're saying is that I'll propose a 20 percent enrollment reduction. If Lance balks, I'll tell him that the six of us will be leaving."

"What do you think he'll say?"

"I doubt he'll put up a fight. He's all about the numbers, and we're the highest-priced talent around here."

"So if we leave, how's Lance going to know who to cut and who to keep?" Barb asked.

"He won't," Bob said.

"So how do we make sure we take our best people with us?" Tom asked.

"I suggest we each make a short list of the people we can't do without and be ready to reach out to those folks as soon as tomorrow morning," Bob said.

"Sounds like a plan," Barb said.

Everyone nodded.

"See you all tomorrow," said Bob.

He still looked tired. But now he sprung up out of his chair, as if a weight had been lifted from his shoulders.

The Beauty Inside

He pushed his way through the revolving door, stepped into the hotel lobby and shook off the cold.

"May I help you, sir?" asked a woman behind the reception desk.

"No, thank you," he said, smiling. "I'm just waiting for a guest."

"Make yourself at home," she said, extending her hand toward an ensemble of furniture around a stone fireplace.

"Thank you."

She smiled a small smile. She looked pleased to watch him as he stepped over toward the fireplace.

He set a book of some sort down on the coffee table and turned toward the fireplace. The hinged glass doors were folded open, and orange flames shot up from the spaces between the fake logs. He preferred real fireplaces, but as he rubbed his hands together and warmed himself, he felt grateful for a fire of any kind.

He felt grateful, too, for this opportunity to see Sarah again. How fortunate he felt to have met her last night. How fortunate they were both still in town on business. How fortunate she had agreed to allow him to sketch her portrait tonight.

It was still hard for him to believe their chance meeting over dinner at the bar and to accept how quickly they had felt comfortable with one another. Both had always felt judged by their appearance: he for his movie-star looks, she for her plainness.

Yet in a matter of minutes, they were each able to see something more, something inside. Now he, an office furniture designer who longed to capture the beauty in ordinary things, had a date to sketch a woman who, until last night, had never really felt beautiful.

"Hello, Michael," she said softly.

"Hello, Sarah," he said, turning to her.

They embraced. It was the first time. Last night, he said good night from the back seat of the taxi they shared, dropping her at her hotel. It was a wonderful evening. But it had seemed too soon for a kiss on the lips, so they both leaned in and gave each other a kiss on the cheek.

Now it felt good to embrace her. Her body felt thin, but her arms felt strong as she wrapped them tightly around his torso.

"Thank you for coming," she said quietly.

"My pleasure," he said softly.

They stood there facing each other, still holding one another. Her green eyes sparkled like emeralds in the firelight. She wore a look of deep contentment.

He had an urge to kiss her on the lips, but he resisted.

She looked over at the coffee table beside him.

"I see you've brought your sketchbook," she said.

"Well, you know I have an eye for beauty."

She blushed.

"I thought we might grab a bite to eat first," she said.

"I'd love to. Do you like Italian?"

"Yes."

"Good. I know a great Italian place a few blocks away."

"Sounds good."

"It's pretty cold," he said. "Would you like to take a cab?"

"I'm up for walking if you are."

"Sure."

She was wearing a long, dark blue coat and a white scarf. She pulled on gloves and a head band that covered her ears. *You look adorable*, he thought.

He picked up his sketch pad. He seldom wore a hat or gloves and hadn't brought any tonight.

"All set?" he asked.

"Yes," she said.

He held the door for her and followed her outside.

"To the right," he said.

As she turned, he extended his left elbow, and she grabbed his arm. He slid his left hand into his coat pocket to keep it warm and, in the process, drew her in closer to him. The way she held tight to his arm suggested she didn't mind.

They walked close together down Nicollet Avenue to a high-rise with a terracotta facade called the Medical Arts Building. They ducked inside. There, on the first floor, was a restaurant named Zelo.

They walked over to the entrance, and he opened the door for her. The sweet aroma of Italian cooking greeted them from inside.

"Smells wonderful," she said.

"Yes, it does," he said.

"May I help you?" asked a pretty young woman from behind the host stand.

"Yes," he said. "We'd like a table for two."

"Do you have a reservation?"

"No, we don't," he answered.

She looked down at her chart.

"I'll have a table open in about 20 minutes. Would that be okay?"

He looked at Sarah. She smiled and nodded.

"Yes," he said.

"Very good. May I have a name, please?"

The host looked up at him, getting a good look at his face for the first time. She smiled.

"Michael."

"Okay, Michael," she said, now staring at his face.

"We'll have a seat at the bar," he said. "If that will be okay."

"What?" the host asked. "Oh, yes. That will be fine. Here's a pager. We'll call when your table's ready."

"Thank you," he said.

She watched him step over to the bar.

"Care for a drink?" he asked Sarah.

"Sure," she said.

The bar was impressive. He didn't drink much, but he was drawn to bars, especially those with vibrant colors and clean lines, like this one. There were three tall columns of glass shelves devoted to color-coded bottles of liquor and a fourth column devoted to wine, red below and white above. Behind the shelves were large glass windows open to the street. The movement of people and cars outside cast shadows and flickers of light across the bottles, like a film. *Surely whoever designed this bar*, he thought, *had all this in mind.*

"Do you ever get used to that?" Sarah asked, taking off her gloves and headband.

"What?"

"Women ogling you."

"Well, I still notice, if that's what you mean."

She decided not to press.

"May I get you two a drink?" the bartender asked.

"What would you like, Sarah?"

What I'd like, she thought, *is hearing you say my name.*

"I'd like a glass of your house cab," she said.

"Same for me, please."

"Very good," the bartender said. "I'll be right back with your wine."

He turned and scanned the place. Light-gray stucco walls. High doorways with flowing arches. Large, rectangular pillars with deep crown molding, behind which soft light radiated upward. Walnut flooring. Walnut paneling nearly halfway up the walls. Clear globe chandeliers. White tablecloths. Brown chairs with black leather cushions.

She noticed him checking everything out.

"Do you approve?"

"Yes," he smiled. "I'm sorry. I didn't mean to ignore you."

"So what type of decor do you like?" she asked.

"I like anything simple."

For the first time in her life, she considered her simple looks a plus.

"Here you are," said the bartender, setting down their glasses of wine. "Will you be dining with us this evening?"

"Yes," Michael said.

"Excellent. Would you like me to have your drink order added to your bill?"

"Yes," Michael said. "That would be fine."

Michael and Sarah lifted their glasses.

"Cheers," she said.

"Cheers."

They clinked their glasses and smiled at each other.

"So there's something I meant to ask you last night," Sarah said, setting her glass on the bar.

"What's that?"

"Do you have a last name?"

"Sorry," he said, smiling. "I guess that would be nice to know. It's Capella."

"That's a beautiful name."

"Thank you."

"Is it Italian?"

"Yes."

A blue-eyed Italian, she thought. *Go figure.*

"What about you?" he asked.

"O'Maley."

"Not Italian."

"Not at all," she said, smiling. "Have you been to Italy?"

"Twice," he said. "Once when I was a boy, to visit my grandparents. And once after I graduated from college. I spent the summer there."

"Visiting your grandparents?"

"No, they were gone by then."

"I'm sorry."

"How about you? Have you been to Ireland?"

"No. But I'd love to go someday."

"You will," he said, with a certainty that surprised her.

Their pager began vibrating and flashing on the bar.

"I guess our table is ready," he said.

As they got up, he pulled a bill from his wallet and laid it on the bar. They stepped over to the host stand, taking their glasses of wine with them.

"Hello again, Michael," the host said. "Your table is ready. Jennifer will seat you."

Sarah watched as the host stared at Michael. She looked pleased when he didn't seem to notice.

"Right this way," Jennifer said.

Michael pulled Sarah's chair out for her and gently pushed it in as she sat down. She liked his manners.

"I see you both have a drink," Jennifer said. "Would you like to hear our specials?"

"Yes, please," Sarah said.

Jennifer went over the specials, looking at Michael nearly the whole time. He kept looking over at Sarah and grinning. This made her feel a little better.

Last evening, when they met, they had each shared a bit about themselves. He told her he had always loved to draw and ended up designing office furniture for high-end clients. She told him she had always loved numbers and ended up as a computer troubleshooter.

They had shared more too, more about themselves. He told her that his good looks had always led people to misjudge him as a lightweight, a pretty boy, and how this frustrated him. She told him that she too felt judged by her looks, how her love of math intimidated guys. She even divulged that she had never had a date. That's when he asked if he could sketch her portrait tonight. When she said yes, he said, "It's a date."

Now she looked across the table at him. His olive skin. His blue eyes. His strong jaw. His long, black, curly hair. Something was different from yesterday. He had shaved! No more stubble. She was surprised she hadn't noticed it earlier.

"What's wrong?" he asked, sensing her surprise.

"You shaved."

"It's a special occasion," he said, smiling.

Clean-shaven, she thought, *he looked even more handsome, if that was possible.*

Jennifer returned.

"Do you know what you'd like?" Sarah asked.

"Yes. I'm going with the tortiglioni rossa. How did you know?"

"You licked your lips when you heard it," she said, smiling.

"I didn't think you noticed," he said, sounding sheepish.

"I'll have the same," Sarah said, looking up at Jennifer, who was staring at Michael.

"Okay," said Jennifer, finally looking at Sarah. "I'll put that order in and have your food out shortly."

When she had left, Michael asked Sarah if she liked tortiglioni rossa.

"I've never had it. But I figured with an Italian man like you, I can't go wrong."

"I'd like to think that too," he smiled.

He wanted to reach across the table and hold her hand. But again, he resisted.

"So where do you live?" he asked.

"Raleigh, North Carolina."

"Is that where you're from?"

"No. I grew up in Cleveland."

"I thought I detected a little accent. What brought you to Raleigh?"

"My job. How about you? Where do you live?"

"I live in Chicago."

"And where are you from?"

"Chicago. I live in a place called Lincoln Park, about 45 minutes from where I grew up."

So they began getting to know each other a bit better.

She shared that her dream was to settle down somewhere and teach math at the grade school level. She had tried to tutor college students in math years before, but she wasn't ready for it. Now she had grown more comfortable working with people, and she had always loved children. And she had grown weary of traveling for business and feeling as if she were simply part of her customers' service contracts. She had loved math as a kid, and now she wanted to help other kids learn to love it too.

He shared that his dream was to own an interior design firm. He liked his job well enough, though he too was tiring of all the travel. His clients had big budgets for their office designs, and when it came to furnishings, most of them wanted more. But he had a passion for simplicity. He wanted to work with clients, especially those on limited budgets, who would appreciate the beauty of a more minimalist touch.

They talked over dinner for three hours, each drawn in by the other's story, when they realized the restaurant was nearly empty.

"Do you still have time for a sketch tonight?" Sarah asked.

"Well, we both need to catch flights pretty early," Michael said. "How about next time?"

"Next time?" Sarah replied hopefully.

"How about if I come visit you in Raleigh sometime?"

He hoped he was not being presumptuous.

"Would you do that?"

"I'd love to."

"Well, then," she smiled. "It's a date."

#

It was a little past noon. His flight was scheduled to land at one, but she wanted to make sure she was there to greet him when he arrived. So she stood in the welcome area in terminal one of the Raleigh-Durham airport. All the seats were taken. She didn't mind standing.

His flight arrived a bit early. She spotted him in the distance. He was walking in a crowd, but her eyes were fixed on him. She saw no one else.

For four weeks, she had thought of little but him. They had been in touch daily. She could hardly believe it. They were an unlikely pair. She, a plain-looking math geek who had never had a date, and he, a gorgeous man with an eye for beauty. She still had a hard time comprehending it.

For four weeks, she had looked forward to seeing him again, but her logical mind told her not to get ahead of herself. They had, after all, been on exactly one date. She figured the odds of this working out were low in the extreme.

But now, seeing him again, she threw logic out the window. She ran to him, past the "Do Not Cross" line, and embraced him.

"Well, hello, Sarah!" he said, seeming a bit surprised by her enthusiasm.

She held him tight. She couldn't let go. Tears welled unexpectedly in her eyes. She had never felt this way before. She was filled with joy.

At last, she loosened her embrace enough to stand back from Michael, to see him. As tears ran down her cheeks, she felt embarrassed. *What must he think of me*, she wondered. She felt like running away, but he took her hands into his. He looked at her face, into her eyes, and smiled.

"You look beautiful, Sarah."

That was all he said, all he needed to say. He spoke words she had dreamed of hearing. She felt as if she were in a dream. She could sense people moving around her, but she could see only him—his face, his smile, his eyes. She felt safe and whole and loved.

"Should we go?" he asked at last.

"Yes," she said. "Yes, let's go."

He picked up his carry-on bag with his left hand and extended his right elbow. She wrapped both of her hands around his right arm, and they walked back through the terminal together.

"Are you hungry?" she asked.

"Famished."

"Do you feel like pub food?"

"Do you mean an Irish pub?" he said, smiling.

"Of course."

"Sarah, I've never been to Raleigh. I'm in your capable hands."

She sure liked the sound of that.

They got into her car in the parking garage and drove to an Irish pub and restaurant called Trali, about 10 minutes from the airport.

"I like this place," she said. "I usually grab a bite here when I land in the evening after a long trip. It reminds me of an Irish pub in Cleveland."

"On your recommendation," he said.

"Well, the food is pretty good, although I'm not sure you'll think much of the decor. It could use a designer's touch."

"Maybe I'll open an office in Raleigh," he said.

That would be nice, she thought.

They ordered club sandwiches, chips and her favorite beer, Smithwick's Irish Ale.

"To Ireland," she said, raising her glass.

"To *visiting* Ireland," he said with a smile.

"I've made a reservation at a restaurant which I think will be much more to your liking this evening," she said.

"Sounds great."

"I wasn't sure what you might want to do this afternoon."

"Any suggestions?"

Oh yeah, she thought. *A king size bed in a hotel room came to mind.* Instead, she said, "We have a pretty nice museum of modern art here."

"I'd love to see that."

"Would you like to check into your hotel first?"

"No, that's okay. I can check in after our tour, before dinner."

"Okay."

He's so easy to be with, she thought.

After lunch, they drove to the Contemporary Art Museum of Raleigh.

"It's really a museum about art *and* design," she said. "I thought you'd especially like the design part."

"Thank you," he said. "I'm sure I will."

There were four featured exhibitions, two devoted to art and two devoted to design. Naturally, Michael was more interested in the design exhibitions.

The first one they looked at featured houses, commercial buildings and other structures designed by Frank Lloyd Wright. Michael was thrilled. He had always loved the vision and craftsmanship of Wright's work, especially his interior designs. He had visited Fallingwater, the Guggenheim Museum and, of course, Wright's many buildings in Chicago.

For Sarah, it was like having her own docent. She loved seeing how Michael's eyes, and his whole face, lit up when he explained what Wright was trying to do with a particular ceiling beam, doorway or piece of furniture. It was as if someone had turned on a light inside him.

The next exhibition was devoted to the design of machinery. Sarah had seen it online but hadn't mentioned it to Michael because she thought he might consider it boring. She was pleasantly surprised to see that he seemed as drawn to it as he was to Wright's work.

He was particularly fascinated by a piece which featured a dozen metal gears lined up along a metal track, their cogs meshed together. Each gear was a different color, and the colors blended naturally, one to the next. He stared at it, studied it, walked all around the display.

"Do you like it?" she asked.

"I love it," he said.

"Why?"

"Just look at it," he said. "Gears. What could be more ordinary? What could be more functional? But they're such a thing of beauty. Who would have thought something so ordinary, so functional could be so beautiful?"

And then he looked up at her and smiled.

"I love ... the way you see things," she said.

When they were finished with the machinery exhibition, they browsed the pieces and displays in the two art exhibitions. But neither of them captured his interest like the design exhibitions.

"Would you like to take off?" she asked.

"I'm ready when you are."

They headed downtown. He was staying at the Sheraton, just a few blocks from her apartment.

"I'll pick you up in an hour," she said, pulling up to the entrance of his hotel.

"Okay."

"Don't forget your sketchbook," she said.

"I won't," he promised.

When she came back, he was standing outside the front door of the hotel, wearing a blue sport coat, a white dress shirt and black jeans but no overcoat. It was late February and, to her, it was bitterly cold. But he didn't seem to mind the cold, which is probably why he never wore a hat or gloves. Standing there, he looked like a model. She was particularly delighted to see he was holding his sketchbook.

She took him to the Capital Grille, about 15 minutes away.

"I know it's a chain," she said. "But the food is great, and I think you'll like the bar and the simple design. Clean lines."

She's really getting me, he thought.

They decided to order the same meals as they had at Julian's, where they met. He ordered salmon and white wine, and she ordered filet mignon and red wine. Just like at Julian's, after seeing her filet, Michael regretted his choice. She noticed and, just like at Julian's, cut him a generous slice.

It was a small thing, but it made them both feel they were really getting to know one another.

They talked over dinner for several hours.

"Are you still up for that sketch?" she asked hopefully. "I know you need to leave in the morning."

"Sure," he said. "If you are."

Are you kidding, she thought.

"Sure," she said.

She lived on the second floor of an old building made up of newly renovated loft apartments. Michael liked her place from the moment she flipped on the light. The decor was spare and clean, with large windows, exposed brick walls, reclaimed wood floors and relatively few pieces of contemporary furniture.

She watched him checking things out.

"I just moved in and haven't had a lot of time to do much furnishing," she said.

"Sarah, it's perfect. I love what you've done. I wouldn't add a thing."

"Really?"

The truth is she had no eye for design and had given up on buying furniture, in part to save money.

"Yeah, really. I love your taste."

"Well, thank you. Would you like a drink?"

"No, thanks. I've had enough to drink tonight."

"Well, can I take your jacket?"

"Sure," he said, taking it off and handing it to her, after removing several pencils from the inside pocket.

She hung it in a closet near the door along with her own heavy coat.

Michael was standing in the middle of the main room, holding his sketchbook and pencils.

"May I sketch you?"

"I thought you'd never ask," she said playfully. "Where would you like me? Uh, to sit. Where would you like me to sit?"

He smiled and looked around the room. He spotted a wooden, ladder-back chair. He stepped over to it.

"Would you be comfortable sitting on this? It should take me only about 15 minutes. We can put a pillow on the seat if you like."

"That should work fine," she said. "Where is best?"

"Do you have a kitchen chair?"

"Yes," she said, heading into the kitchen, which was open to the main room.

"Here, I'll get that," he said, following her.

"Thank you," he said, taking the chair from her. He carried it into the main room and set it about five feet across from the other chair.

"There," he said. "Just close enough to see you but far enough that I won't accidentally stick you with a pencil."

She laughed.

"Am I wearing the right thing?" she asked, hoping he might ask her to take something off.

"You might take off your sweater, if you're comfortable."

If you're comfortable. He seemed to use that phrase a lot. It felt good to have someone who cared about her comfort.

"Okay," she said. "Let me slip this off. I'll be right back."

She disappeared through one of only two visible doors. He assumed it was the door to her bedroom.

He stepped over to the kitchen chair and laid his sketchbook and pencils on the seat. A minute later, Sarah re-emerged, without her sweater. As she stepped over to her chair and got close to him, he caught a whiff of fresh perfume.

"Just let me know how you'd like me to pose," she said.

"Don't pose," he said. "Just sit naturally, like you would if we were simply sitting here talking."

She sat down, and he took his seat across from her.

"Do you have enough light?" she asked.

"Plenty," he said, opening his sketchbook and setting it on his thighs. "The lighting is perfect."

"Should I smile?" she asked.

"Yes."

"Do your subjects usually smile?"

"Sometimes. But I just like it when you smile. It makes your face light up."

You make my face light up, she thought.

"There," he said. "That's perfect. Stay just like that, if you can. And you don't have to keep smiling."

Oh yes, I do, she thought.

He first sketched an outline of her head and shoulders. Then he switched pencils, first to draw her facial features, then to shade.

As he sketched, he told her again about the things he used to draw in his room as a boy, just as he'd done the night they met: a chair, a desk, a TV, a lamp, a filing cabinet, books on bookshelves, his sister, his brother, his dog.

"It's the ordinary things, Sarah," he said, concentrating on his drawing, "that are the real things of beauty, the true objects of art."

She had always felt ordinary. Now she felt like a thing of beauty.

"There," he said, holding his sketchbook up, facing him. "Finished."

"May I see?" she asked.

"Of course. I hope you like it."

He turned the sketchbook around and held it up at eye level. Her eyes scanned the page. Her jaw dropped, and she covered her mouth with her left hand.

"What do you think?" he asked, hoping she was pleased.

She stared at the sketch and said nothing. She could not speak. It was her, all right. But drawn in a way she had never imagined herself. It was an accurate depiction of her face, but somehow it was more lovely than she had ever seen it, looking in a mirror or at photographs.

"I think it's amazing," she finally said, looking up at him. "It's me, for sure. But I'm not beautiful."

"Oh yes, you are," he said. "I've only sketched what I see when I look at you."

"Michael," she said, looking into his eyes. "You make me feel beautiful."

She stood up. He stood up, dropped his sketchbook and pencils on the floor and took a step toward her.

"Michael," she said.

"Sarah."

He cradled her face in his hands, closed his eyes and leaned into her. Their lips met. They kissed, first softly, then hard. She had never kissed a man like this before.

Finally, they stopped kissing and simply held each other and smiled, looking into one another's eyes. She knew she was falling in love with this man, but dare she tell him? Was it too soon? Might it scare him off?

He brushed her hair back from the sides of her face and gently stroked her cheeks with his fingers.

"Sarah?"

"Yes?"

"I love you."

She felt weak.

"Oh, Michael. I love you too."

They were words she had never heard from any man or uttered to any man but her father.

They were words he had heard from many women but had never uttered to any woman but his mother. He knew these women all wanted him to say I love you in return, but he also knew they did not really love him. They barely knew him. In fact, Sarah was first woman he had dated more than once. She was the only one who could see beyond his looks, who could see him on the inside.

They held each other and kissed a while longer and said I love you again. She wasn't sure where all of this would lead.

Then he surprised her by saying, "I would love to stay, but I think I should be going."

They were words she did not want to hear. Her spirit longed to be with this man, and her body ached for him. But her mind told her he was probably right.

"Will you have time to meet me for breakfast?" she asked hopefully.

"Absolutely," he said.

She went to the closet and got his jacket.

"Don't forget your sketchbook," she said.

"Please keep it. I hope to have the privilege of sketching you again."

"You will," she said, giving him a long, soulful kiss. "And the privilege will be mine."

#

They had spoken by phone every day for three weeks. They were really getting to know each other, but talking by phone only made them want to be together even more.

Now Sarah was walking through terminal three in O'Hare airport. Ahead, in the distance, she could make out Michael's outline.

They rushed together. She could not contain herself. She jumped into his arms, wrapping her arms around his neck, and he held her there, suspended, as they kissed and traded hellos. At last, he put her down. She looked up and saw tears running down his cheeks. She had never seen a man cry, at least not in person.

"I'm sorry," he said, wiping his tears away. "It's just that I've missed you so much."

"I understand," she said softly. "I've missed you too."

Knowing she would need to leave in the morning, Michael had planned a few things to make the most of her brief stay, things he thought they both would like.

First, lunch at an authentic Irish pub named Lizzie O'Neill's, overlooking the Chicago River. Next, a quick trip to Oak Park to tour Frank Lloyd Wright's home and studio. Then a drive to her hotel downtown so she could check in and freshen up for dinner at one of his favorite Italian restaurants, Sapori Trattoria, near his apartment in Lincoln Park.

Michael waited for Sarah in the hotel lobby. A beautifully lit stone and metal wall-fountain caught his eye. It was his kind of design, a perfect blend of nature and human engineering, reminiscent of Wright's work.

Yet as striking as that fountain was, his mind was somewhere else. It was on Sarah. He had never met anyone like her. She was so real and unassuming. That alone was attractive to him, but beyond that, she seemed so intensely interested in him. Not just his outward appearance, but who he really was. It moved him. He never cried, and yet he had cried at the sight of her at the airport. She was beautiful—not in a classic sense or in a way anyone but he might see—but in her plainness, he saw elegance. He knew he might never find another woman like this. He also knew she would be leaving in the morning, that he would not see her again for a while. The very thought of being apart from her made him sad. He wanted to be with her.

"Ready, Michael?"

He looked up, and there she was, in a navy blue, soft knit dress. He had never seen her in a dress.

"Sarah, you look lovely."

"Well, thank you, Michael," she said, blushing.

"May I escort you?" he asked, extending his left elbow.

"Of course," she giggled, clutching his arm.

They both had the Cappellacci all'Aragosta. She ordered it because it reminded her of his last name, and she loved hearing him pronounce it.

For three hours, they took turns sharing more about their lives. Stories from their childhoods. Their hopes and fears. Each of them felt comfortable letting the other see more deeply inside.

Finally, he asked, "Would you like to go back to my place for a nightcap?"

I thought you'd never ask, she thought.

"I'd love that," she said.

He opened the door to his apartment and flipped on the light. Like Sarah's place, it was a loft apartment. Like Sarah's, it was uncluttered, with wood floors, exposed brick walls and contemporary furniture. But there was something different here. Sarah had not put much thought or time into how her place looked. From the moment she stepped into Michael's place, she could tell he had paid careful attention to how everything fit together: the spaces between things, the blend of textures, the vibrant colors. It was as if she were looking at a painting.

"I love your place," she said.

"Thanks. It's okay for now, I guess."

"It's you."

He smiled.

"Would you like a drink?"

"Sure."

"What would you like?"

"Whatever you're having."

"Well, I've been saving a bottle of Tenuta San Guido Sassicaia for a special occasion."

She loved how the Italian seemed to roll off his tongue. She smiled, admiring a Van Gogh of a field of red poppies, hung on the wall over the red sofa.

"Is this a special occasion?" she asked.

"I sure hope so," he said.

She turned around. Michael was down on one knee, looking up at her, holding a small box, opened with a diamond ring in it.

"Sarah, will you marry me?"

Well-Being

I woke up. I couldn't speak or see. But I could hear a woman's voice.

"Mr. Douglas. Can you hear me?"

"Yes," I mumbled, barely able to move my lips.

I heard someone gasp.

"Mr. Douglas. Can you open your eyes?"

My eyelids felt like sand bags, but I wanted to see. Raising my eyebrows, with all the strength I had in the muscles of my forehead, I slowly opened my eyes.

In the dim light, I could see two women, dressed in white, looking down at me. I was lying in bed, and they were standing at my sides.

"Mr. Douglas," said the one on the left. "Can you hear me?"

"Yes," I said, more clearly this time. "And I can see you now too."

The two women looked at each other, as if they were not sure what to say.

"Where am I?" I asked.

"You're in a room in a 500 ward in sector four," said the woman on the right.

"Brenda!" said the woman on the left, sounding irritated. "He's not going to know what that means. Let me handle this."

I looked up at the woman on the left.

"Mr. Douglas, my name is Cathy. Brenda and I are your nurses here. You've been asleep, in a coma actually, for a very long time."

"How long?" I asked.

"Five hundred years," Cathy said.

"Five hundred years!" I cried. "That's impossible! Where am I? Where is my wife? Where are my children?"

"Mr. Douglas," Cathy said. "Let me explain. Five hundred years ago, you were in a car accident. You were brought to a hospital near here. The surgeons were able to save your life, but you slipped into a coma and never regained consciousness. Until now."

I blinked and looked around. I was in a bed with my head and back slightly raised. A plastic tube was taped to my right arm, which looked so thin. Another tube protruded from under the thin blanket which covered me. Both tubes were connected to a device at the foot of my bed. I could see nothing else in the room except two straight-backed chairs, which I assumed belonged to the nurses.

"Where am I?" I asked. "What is this place?"

Brenda looked at Cathy, who nodded.

"Mr. Douglas," said Brenda. "The world is very different from the one you've known. It's going to take time for you to fully understand the changes, but let me start with the basics."

"Okay," I said.

"First, you no longer live in the United States because that country, like all countries from your time, no longer exists. The world is now divided into sectors. We are in sector four."

"Sectors?"

"Yes. They were designated about 300 years ago. There are 12 sectors in all."

"Why sectors?"

"They were decreed by the tribunal after the great redistribution."

"The what?"

"Mr. Douglas," said Cathy, waving Brenda off. "Let's step back for a moment. When you had your accident, there were seven and a half billion people in the world. Half of the world's wealth was owned by one percent of those people. About 30 percent of people in the world were overweight or obese. About 13 percent were starving. About half the world had no access to health care. Our planet was warming at an alarming rate. And we were on the brink of blowing ourselves up with nuclear weapons."

"The world was a mess," Brenda chimed in.

Cathy looked annoyed.

"Yes," Cathy continued. "People had had enough. They realized that we were on a path to self-destruction. So they began to demand major reforms. But governments weren't willing to make the kinds of reforms people were after, so the people banded together and took control. They dissolved their national constitutions and set up a tribunal to oversee a new world order. Are you with me so far, Mr. Douglas?"

"I'm not sure," I said. "Can you give me a few examples of how the world is now?"

"Certainly," said Cathy, looking at Brenda and nodding.

"Mr. Douglas," said Brenda. "Let me start by telling you that our mantra is well-being. Well-being for everyone and everything on our planet."

"Well-being?"

"Yes," Brenda continued. "It has fallen to all of us to take care of every man, woman and child on Earth as well as the Earth itself."

"How do we do that?" I asked.

"It's simple, really," Brenda said. "For example, every person is given enough food to ensure an adequate number of calories a day and in the right nutritional balance."

"That alone is a big change," Cathy chimed in.

Now Brenda looked at Cathy.

"Sorry," Cathy said. "Go ahead."

"Income is capped so that a living wage is enjoyed by all. All income is taxed at 15 percent. All tax revenue is shared to pay for ways to enhance the well-being of people everywhere."

"Such as?" I asked.

"Food, shelter, security, education, health care and renewable energy," Brenda said. "These are our common priorities."

"But if people can only make a living wage, is there enough money to go around?"

"Plenty. Partly because people need far less these days. And partly because there are fewer people."

"Fewer?"

"Far fewer," Brenda said. "The world's population is back down to six billion, and we're managing growth carefully."

I didn't have the strength to ask how the population was kept in check. So I simply asked, "How is it working?"

"Very well," Cathy said. "You yourself are a living example of the benefits of the advances we've made in health care."

"How so?" I asked.

"When you had your accident," said Cathy, "the average life-span of a man in the United States was about 78 years. Now, we're not even sure what the upward limit is."

"What do you mean?" I asked.

"Well," said Brenda, "for example, you are now 542 years old, Mr. Douglas. And I must say you are still in remarkably good health."

"You mean there are others as old as me?"

"Not many," Cathy said. "You're one of the oldest people on Earth. But given the pace of the advancement of our genomic and health care technologies, there is no reason to set an upward limit on life expectancy."

I blinked.

"Where am I? I mean what kind of a place is this?"

"You are in a special facility dedicated to the care of people who have reached their 500th year," Brenda said.

"In sector four," Cathy added.

"What do people like me do here?" I asked.

The two nurses looked at each other.

"Nothing really," Cathy said.

"Nothing?" I asked.

"That's right," Brenda said. "You worked hard as a young man, Mr. Douglas. You provided for your family, and you paid taxes. If would be unfair for us not to take care of you now, just as we would take care of anyone."

"Anyone?" I asked.

"Yes, anyone," Cathy said. "That's the idea. Equality in every way."

"Total equality," Brenda added.

I was having a hard time understanding.

"Where is my wife?" I asked. "Where are my children?"

The nurses looked at each other.

"Your wife and children are gone, Mr. Douglas," Cathy said. "I am sorry."

"Gone? When?"

"They died more than 400 years ago," Brenda said. "Unlike you, they were not able to benefit from the medical advances we've made over the past 500 years. Unfortunately, they died too soon. They were among the last of the pre-tribunal era people, before we could get everything organized and everyone in the system."

"I am sorry, Mr. Douglas," Cathy said.

It seemed I had just kissed my wife and children goodbye that morning. I missed them. My eyes welled with tears.

"Then why am I still alive?"

"You survived in a coma just long enough to begin to receive DNA infusions," Cathy said. "DNA from your younger self, Mr. Douglas. We were able to take samples of your DNA when you were in your sixties. We inject it back into your system periodically. That's why you'll continue to be in your sixties, possibly forever."

"Forever?"

"Well, yes, theoretically," Brenda said.

"But I don't want to live like this forever!"

The nurses looked at each other quizzically.

"Mr. Douglas," Cathy said. "You are in relatively good health. We give you proper nutrition every day. You want for nothing because others pay for everything you need. The Earth is cooling. Our air and water are clean. And the world is at peace. What more could you ask for?"

I looked back and forth at the nurses. I looked more closely at their faces. They were flawless. I could not tell their age.

"But I'm not *supposed* to live here forever! My wife and children are gone. I should be gone too. I should be with them."

"But Mr. Douglas," Cathy said. "You are not with them. You are here, with us."

"And it is our duty, Mr. Douglas," Brenda said, adjusting a dial on the device at the foot of my bed, "to ensure your well-being."

Presence

Anthony first smoked when he was five. He got drunk the first time when he was six. He started shoplifting when he was seven. He had sex when he was 10. He couldn't fully perform. But she could. She was 12.

By the time he was 11, he had gotten into so many fights at school that he was expelled. At 12, he tried to rape a 10-year-old girl. While he was being held in jail, he tried to hang himself. When his mother didn't show up to post bail, he was released into the custody of the county and admitted to a juvenile detention center.

That's where he met James, who had just started an internship there. He was a junior in college.

A few days after Anthony was admitted, James' supervisor, a woman named Marjorie, approached James to ask him if he would work with Anthony.

"What's his situation?" he asked.

"This is a tough case," she said.

"How tough?"

"This kid has been in trouble his whole life."

"What kind of trouble?"

"Well, last week, he tried to rape a girl. A few days ago, he tried to kill himself."

"Sounds like he needs some serious help."

"He's getting it. He's seeing our best psychiatrist, but he needs more. He needs someone he can talk with."

"Marjorie, you know I don't have any real experience in this."

"Just talk with him, James. If you decide it's too much, I'll find someone else."

"Okay."

"Thank you," she said. "I'll arrange for a meeting in the morning."

#

Anthony was sitting on a bench under a maple tree in a small courtyard bordered by the brick walls of the U-shaped center as James approached him.

The boy looked much older than 12. His face was worn and drawn. His eyes were deep-set, with dark circles under them. His coarse hair splayed out, long and wild. He looked like a stray dog.

"Good morning, Anthony. My name is James Cook."

He extended his hand, but the boy didn't take it or even look at him. James didn't say anything. Instead, he simply asked, "May I sit down?" The boy didn't answer, at least not verbally, but he did look down at the space on the bench next to him. James took it as a sign of engagement and sat down.

"So when did you get here?" James asked.

Anthony rolled his eyes. "Man, you know when I got here."

"You're right. I do know. You got here four days ago."

"Then why did you ask?" chopping his hand into the air.

"Because I was wondering how, being here for four days, you've managed to escape getting a haircut."

"You gotta be shittin' me, man."

"I wouldn't do that, Anthony."

"Well, whatta ya mean then? You think I'm a mess?"

"No, I didn't say that."

"What then?"

"I think you need a haircut, that's all. You need a haircut badly."

"Is that so?"

"Yeah."

"You gonna cut it for me, big man?"

"Yeah, I'll cut it for you, Anthony."

The boy didn't believe him.

"Where you gonna do that?"

"There's a barber shop inside."

"It's closed."

"I can get the key."

"Man, you're shitting me," he said, looking away and shaking his head.

"Anthony, I told you. I wouldn't do that."

"Okay, big man. You're on. But you better know what you're doin'."

James had never cut anyone's hair in his life. But he saw an opening with the boy, and he took it.

The barber shop didn't open until noon. It was not even 10. James got the key from the front desk, then stopped by Marjorie's office to make sure this would be okay. She was surprised but said yes and reminded James to keep the door open — center policy.

"Be careful in there," she called after him.

"I'll be fine," he said.

"I'm talking to Anthony," she said, smiling.

James unlocked the door and flipped on the lights.

"Your hair looks dirty, Anthony. We're going to need to wash it before I can cut it."

"Screw you, man."

"Anthony, that's the deal. And watch your language."

James didn't know if he was pushing too hard, but he stepped over to the sink and turned the water on, running his hand under it to test the temperature. Out of the corner of his eye, he was pleasantly surprised to see Anthony sitting down in a chair in front of the sink.

"That chair tilts back."

"I know, man," the boy said, fumbling with a lever on the side. The chair lurched back, and he nearly slammed the back of his head into the sink.

"Be careful," James said. "Let me put a towel around your neck before you sit back."

He draped a white cotton hand towel around Anthony's neck, slipped his hand under the back of his head, and lowered it into a curved notch in the edge of the sink. He thought the boy might resist. Instead, he closed his eyes and sat still, with his hands folded on his lap.

James pulled the nozzle from its mount, pressed a button on the handle and sprayed the boy's hair, smoothing it with his hand.

"Is that water temperature okay?"

"It's fine. It's good."

James turned off the water, grabbed a bottle of shampoo and began working it into Anthony's hair.

"That okay?"

"Feels funny."

"Funny?" He looked down. James had a small smile on his face.

"Yeah. Ain't nobody ever washed my hair before."

"Now, Anthony. I find that hard to believe. You're telling me your mom never washed your hair when you were little?"

"If she did, I don't remember."

"What's your earliest memory?"

At first, Anthony didn't respond. He's ignoring me, James thought.

But then, with his eyes still closed, he said, "The first thing I remember is getting whipped."

"Who whipped you, Anthony?"

"My mom."

James turned the water back on and began rinsing Anthony's hair. Neither of them said anything. Then James grabbed a towel and gently rubbed the boy's hair until it was semi-dry.

"Okay, Anthony," James said, lifting his neck and helping him sit up. "Let's cut your hair."

Anthony walked over to a swivel chair and sat down. James spotted a short stack of small, folded sheets. He grabbed one and draped it around Anthony's neck. The chair was too low, so James raised it by pumping a pedal underneath.

Then he looked up and saw the reflection of himself and the boy in the mirror. Anthony was looking at James' face. Up to that point, he had not made eye contact. Now, he was at least looking at his face, if only indirectly. James took this as a good sign.

"How do you like your hair cut, Anthony?"

"Short."

"Same length all over?"

"Yeah."

"Well, then, we'll give you a buzz cut," James said, picking up a trimmer. No scissors, he thought. Thank God. He'd had a close-cropped beard the winter before and knew how to use a trimmer, at least on his own face.

"I'll use a number four," James said, snapping on a clipper guard. "That's pretty short. But if you want to go even shorter, we can do that."

"What about you?"

"What about me, Anthony?"

"Was you whipped when you were a kid?"

"No, Anthony. I wasn't. My parents never hit me."

"You had a mom and a dad?"

"Yep. Still do. What about you?"

"My mom's not around much. I never seen my dad."

James clicked on the trimmer. As he began to cut Anthony's hair, in the privacy of the barber shop, over the whirr of the trimmer, the boy began to tell him about his life. How he couldn't remember a time when he wasn't in trouble for something. How he felt alone in the world. How he was afraid he'd end up in a place like this.

James listened and began to tell Anthony about himself too. How he grew up in a big house. How he planned to become a financial adviser, like his father. How he was at the center only because a semester of "community service" was required at school.

For Anthony, it was the first time he had ever talked about his life, the first time anyone had even seemed interested.

For James, it was a huge surprise. He was a "numbers guy" and had signed up for this internship as a check-the-box exercise. And yet here he was, watching a perfect stranger go from being unwilling to acknowledge his presence to trusting him to cut his hair, and now beginning to share his story, within the span of an hour. And all he had done was show up.

James finished cutting Anthony's hair. Suddenly, he looked younger. James grabbed a towel and brushed the loose hairs from his head, face and neck.

"How does that look?"

"Great," Anthony replied, smiling and, in the mirror, looking James in the eye. "Thank you."

And with that, the two of them left the barber shop and walked down the hall to the cafeteria, where they continued to talk over lunch, then well into the afternoon.

#

That fall, James worked at the center two days a week, on Tuesdays and Thursdays. On those days, and sometimes on weekends, he came to see Anthony. They would play video games and talk for hours.

Over the course of the semester, Marjorie assigned James a few other children too, to round out his internship. Seeing how close he and Anthony were becoming, and the positive effect it was having, she let James continue to focus on him.

Anthony attended school at the center. He was so far behind that he had to begin with the fourth graders. But now, for the first time in his life, he actually enjoyed going to school. By Christmas, he had caught up with kids his own age. By the following spring, his grades were among the best in his class.

By Christmas, James' internship was complete, but he decided to keep seeing Anthony. In fact, he began to come see him nearly every day. Not because he had to, but because the two of them had become like brothers.

#

Anthony spent another year in the center because his mother took no interest in him and no one else claimed him. He continued doing well in school and ended up graduating from the eighth grade near the top of his class.

The center's policy was to house children for no more than two years. After that, provided they were stable, most kids and teens became candidates for either foster care or adoption.

As Anthony was graduating from eighth grade, James was graduating from college. Several months before he graduated, he accepted a job with the biggest investment firm in town.

Once he graduated, James took Anthony into foster care. A year later, Anthony's mother died of a drug overdose. Three months after that, when Anthony was 16, James adopted him.

#

Anthony was valedictorian of his high school class. He spoke at his graduation. James was sitting in the front row of the parents' section.

"Our lives are filled with moments of great joy, like this one," Anthony said. "But there are moments of despair too, times when we feel alone and afraid and wonder if we can go on. But we will go on because, completely unknown to us, someone is out there, waiting to save us. They will come to us when we least expect it. It will not be dramatic. There will be no soaring music or beating drums. It will happen when you're sitting on a bench or getting your hair cut. But you will know it. You'll feel a new presence in your life, and you will realize that you were never really alone."

Everything is Real

David and Myrna Kaplan didn't survive the crash. But Sam, their eight-year-old daughter who was sitting in the back seat, did.

There were no seat belts in 1952, and she was thrown through the windshield. The collision broke nearly every bone in her body. Yet somehow she was alive when the ambulance arrived. The medics rushed her to Cook County Hospital, where a team of doctors immediately got to work.

They weren't concerned about her bones. Those could be repaired, and eventually they would heal. But one of her lungs was so badly damaged that they had to remove it, and her heart and other lung were in terrible shape.

"She won't make it through the night," said Dr. Thomas, the chief of surgery.

Chicago was being pummeled by a blizzard. It had caused the Kaplans' accident. Sadly, it was the kind of night when a healthy heart or lung might suddenly become available.

However, it seemed Sam's fate was sealed. She had simply been born too soon. Medical journals would not record the first successful human heart-lung transplant for another 29 years.

After eight hours of surgery, Sam's doctors concluded they had done all they could for her. A little after midnight, they turned her over to two operating room nurses, who now had the seemingly impossible task of keeping her alive.

The nurses' names, embroidered on their scrubs, were Barbara Keith and Nell Lohman. Once the doctors left, they stepped over to Sam's bed to wheel her into recovery.

Nell released the brake, but Barbara grabbed the bed frame and held it in place.

"Wait," Barbara said.

Nell looked up at her. Barbara was looking at Sam's heavily bandaged face and holding her right hand. Nell looked down at Sam's face too. Then she reached out and took hold of her other hand. The two of them stood there, gently holding Sam's hands, in silence.

Suddenly the operating room door swung open, and in walked another doctor. He was in scrubs. His mouth and nose were covered. His eyes had the intense look of a man on a mission. "Dr. Simon" was embroidered on his chest pocket. Neither Barbara nor Nell had met Dr. Simon, but they certainly knew his name. He was one of the finest surgeons in the country. He worked at Michael Reese, a research and teaching hospital just a few miles away.

"Good morning, doctor," said Barbara. "Are you here for Sam?"

He nodded. Just then, a second doctor came through the doors, wheeling in a machine unlike anything the nurses had ever seen. A third doctor followed close behind. He was carrying a metal cooler.

Dr. Simon turned toward the nurses.

"Nurse Keith. Nurse Lohman. I know it's late. Would you please assist me in this procedure?"

"Of course, doctor."

"Of course."

They wheeled Sam back to the operating table, lifted her up on it and prepared her for surgery. Dr. Simon administered the anesthesia.

A few minutes later, he re-opened the incision in Sam's chest and spread her ribs, giving him access to her heart and lung. The second doctor then connected her to the machine. Dr. Simon carefully removed the failing organs.

The nurses felt dizzy, not from the blood but from witnessing a procedure they had never seen and would have thought was impossible.

Then the third doctor handed Dr. Simon a donor heart and lung and helped him sew them into place. A few minutes later, the new organs began to warm up, and the lung began to inflate. The heart began to beat rapidly and irregularly. Dr. Simon asked for a paddle. He used it to apply a small electric shock to the heart, which then began beating properly.

With the new organs functioning normally, the second doctor removed the machine. Dr. Simon closed Sam's chest.

"Take good care of this little girl," he said.

Then, as quickly as they had come in, Dr. Simon and his associates left.

#

"How is the patient?" asked Dr. Thomas as he entered the intensive care unit during his morning rounds.

"She's doing fine," said the attending nurse.

"What?"

"Yes, haven't you heard? Dr. Simon removed her ruined heart and lung and put in new ones last night. It's a miracle."

"What?"

"He called it a 'heart-lung transplant'."

"Dr. Simon?"

"Yes, from Michael Reese."

Dr. Thomas left the room and hurried over to the nurses station.

"Nurse, get Dr. Simon at Michael Reese on the phone for me."

"Yes, doctor," she said.

She picked up the phone and dialed the number.

"This is Marilyn Pemberton calling for Dr. Thomas from Cook County Hospital. May I speak with Dr. Simon, please?"

She looked up at Dr. Thomas. There was a voice at the other end of the line.

"Excuse me?" the nurse said, with a look for disbelief on her face. "Are you sure?"

"What is it?" Dr. Thomas asked.

She turned away. "Very well," she said softly. "I'm sorry. Thank you."

She hung up the phone.

"What they did they say?" Dr. Thomas asked.

She looked up.

"They said Dr. Simon and his son were killed in a car accident in the blizzard yesterday afternoon."

#

"Everything you can imagine is real," Picasso said.

People and places, ideas and events, hopes and fears. An extraordinary surgeon who performed one final operation to save a little girl who had been given up for dead by using a machine which had not yet been invented, even as his own obituary was being written.

All we can imagine is real.

Everything is real.

Spring

Through the slightly opened window, he could smell the sweet fragrance of lilacs and dogwood blossoms borne on the warm air from the courtyard below.

At least they allowed him this one connection with the outside world. He guessed they figured that a bedridden old man isn't going to escape, especially from two floors up.

He loved spring. It reminded him of playing baseball as a kid in an empty lot down the street from his house. He loved the feel of the soggy earth beneath his feet. He loved the freedom of shedding his winter coat.

Freedom. It had been so long since he knew what it was like to come and go as he pleased. Now his days were spent in this hospital bed. They served his meals here. They made him swallow his pills here. They changed his diapers here.

He gazed through the window at the setting sun. Soon it would be dark. There would be one more check tonight, then lights out.

He waited until his nurse was gone. She had left his window open just a crack. Maybe she knew how he felt about spring. Had he told her? He couldn't remember.

He pulled back his blanket and sheets, sat up and swung his legs over the side of his bed. His feet dangled well above the floor. He slipped off the bed and came down hard on the bare soles of his feet. A pain shot through his legs, but he resisted calling out. He hoped no one had heard the thud.

He shuffled over to a chair in the corner and sat down, looking around his room from a new vantage point. This was where his visitors sat, although he hadn't had a visitor in a quite a while.

He looked at his bed. To him, it was more like a prison. How strange it seemed to not be lying there now and to see it empty, like a prisoner surveying his vacant cell from the outside. For a moment, he felt like a man again.

The window was now less than two feet away. He could feel the warm breeze on his face. It called to him like spring beckons a child to come out and play.

He knew what he had to do. He stood and slowly made his way back to his bed. He peeled back the blankets, letting them fall on the floor. Then he pulled off the sheets and dragged them back to the chair. Sitting there, in the dim light, his hands shaking, he tied the sheets together, corner to corner.

When he was finished, he flung his newly fashioned "rope" across the linoleum floor to see how long it was. It barely stretched beyond his bed. He knew it was too short. What else could he use?

He thought of the fabric shower curtain in his bathroom. He went in, reached up and unhooked the plastic clips that suspended the curtain from a rod across the shower.

He dragged the curtain back to the chair. Sitting back down, he picked up the end of the string of sheets and tied it to the corner of the shower curtain. Was it long enough now? It would have to be.

He stepped over to the window and cranked it all the way open. He tied one end of his makeshift rope to the handle and tossed the rest over the ledge.

He stepped back over to the chair and pushed it to the wall beneath the window. Grabbing the back of the chair, he pulled himself up, first kneeling, then standing on the seat.

Holding tight to the marble ledge to steady himself, he swung his right leg over it, through the open window frame. Then he raised his left leg and extended it into the open air behind him.

He was now on his belly, his head poking into his room and his legs dangling out of the window. He inched back and grabbed the cloth rope with both hands. He knew he'd have to climb down quickly, that he couldn't hold on very long, so he began his descent.

He tried to ignore the awful pain in his shoulders, the trembling of his arms, the way the coarse brick wall was digging into his skin. He tried not to look down. He tried not to worry if the rope would be long enough.

Instead, he closed his eyes and breathed in the lilacs and felt the warm breeze on his face. He ran down the street to the empty lot and returned to the joy and the freedom of spring.

Part III

Desserts

Magnetic Pull

"Did you know there's a low tide and a high tide every morning and every afternoon?" she asked.

"No," he said, lying on his side next to her in the sand.

"Well, there is. Every six hours and twelve minutes, the tide changes."

"Really?"

He couldn't take his eyes off her. All of her.

"Yep," she said, pretending not to notice. "As the moon waxes and wanes, the tide rises and falls. It all works on the magnetic pull of the moon."

"Magnetic pull, huh?"

"Yep."

He got up on his knees, leaned over and kissed her hard. He couldn't resist.

Doing the Dishes

They were busy professionals. Most days, they barely saw each other. Their marriage felt the strain. Every little thing seemed to be a big deal these days.

So they were really upset when their dishwasher broke and they learned the repair service couldn't get to it for two weeks.

At first, they took turns doing the dishes. Then on Sunday, a rare day off for both of them, they decided he would wash and she would dry.

They began talking in a way they hadn't in a long time. The next day, he called the repair service and canceled their request.

Talker

John always was a talker.

By age two, when most kids are just forming words, John was talking in sentences.

By three, he was memorizing and reciting nursery rhymes.

Growing up, John talked non-stop. He had a way with words too. In grade school, when other kids were playing baseball, John was competing in public speaking contests. He always won.

He spoke at his high school graduation.

In college, John majored in oral communication. Upon graduation, he ran for city council.

Right now, John is on the floor of the Senate, leading a filibuster.

Good Morning

He stopped at the cafe every morning on his way to work. He preferred black coffee, but she was the barista in charge of the fancy coffees there. So when he got there, he always ordered a triple, venti, soy, no-foam latte.

He didn't even drink it. He ordered it because she was the one who made it, and he loved to watch her move. She moved with the confidence of an athlete and the grace of an angel.

Confidence and grace—two things he lacked.

Then one morning, he didn't see her at the cafe. He almost left but decided to order a black coffee to go. As he stepped up to the counter, he saw her out of the corner of his eye. She had been hidden away behind the espresso machine.

She saw him and smiled.

"A triple, venti, soy, no-foam latte?" she asked.

He smiled and said, "Good morning."

Where Are You?

"What do you think it was?" she typed.

"I don't know," he typed in response. "Maybe social media. Maybe the Internet itself."

"Those things were supposed to be the great connectors. They were supposed to bring us closer together."

"Yeah, I know. That's the irony."

"I still can't believe it. How could we be on the brink of extinction?"

"Well, when you don't need to see anyone anymore, when you forget how to talk with people, when you forget what it's like to look into someone's eyes, it's kind of hard to reproduce."

"I guess you're right."

They sat still, staring at their screens.

"Where are you?"

Too Much Noise

"We've determined these two ancient tribes lived alongside each other for years," the archaeologist said. "Then suddenly, they wiped each other out."

"Why?"

"We're not sure. But we have a theory, based on their instruments."

"Instruments?"

"Yes. They stretched animal skins over hollowed-out tree stumps."

"Like drums?"

"Yes."

"But what could drums have to do with their demise?"

"We discovered thousands of worn-out animal skins, preserved in the permafrost, all along the border between these peoples. It appears they bombarded each other with noise. At some point, we suspect, they simply couldn't take it any longer."

One More Story

You head up to British Columbia with 12 other guys for a week of roughing it in Yoho National Park.

You're staying in a hut near Lake Louise. You hike and fish by day and drink and tell tall tales around a wood stove by night.

You hear there are grizzlies and black bears roaming the wilderness. So every third guy in your group carries a cartridge of pepper spray on his belt. This year, that includes you.

In all the years you've been making this trip, you've seen only two bears. They were at least a mile away.

Today the sun was hot, so everyone is wiped out. Tonight, the beer, which has been soaking all day in a nearby stream, is cold. You drink your fair share.

You have to pee. The stern lady on the bus to the trailhead yesterday emphasized the importance of using an outhouse "to protect our environment."

You curse her under your breath as you step out under a fingernail moon and a million stars. You scan the woods with your little flashlight and trudge down a skinny, rutted path toward the stinky outhouse.

You're almost there when you hear a noise, a rustling through the brush. You shine your light in that direction. You see eyes that look like black marbles, set deep in an enormous, hairy head. A griz!

It is less than 30 feet away. It stops. You freeze. You want to

135

scream, but you can't breathe. You think about making a dash for the outhouse, but it's too far away.

You shine the beam of your flashlight into the beast's eyes, hoping to blind it, if only long enough to make your escape. But it shakes its head and growls and starts toward you.

You remember the pepper spray, which is still on your belt. The bear is coming at you. You drop your flashlight. It falls to the ground, illuminating a rock.

The fingers of your right hand feel the pepper spray cartridge in its nylon holster. You slip your index finger through a ring in the plastic top and pull the cartridge up and out, a move you've practiced in the safety of the hut.

You can make out a hulking, shadowy figure, now less than 20 feet away. You feel the Earth move, and you hear a low, menacing growl.

You raise the cartridge and aim it at the dark figure. You pull the trigger.

But nothing happens. You remember there's a safety latch on the top of the ring. Your thumb feels it and pulls it back. You pull the trigger again.

This time, you feel the cartridge vibrate and hear a rush of spray into the darkness.

Then you hear an awful moan, and your nostrils take in something wicked, as the terrible moaning continues.

You half expect to feel a 600-pound bear pounce on you and rip you apart.

But the source of the moaning comes no closer. You hear it coughing and see it pawing at its head.

You make a break for it. You turn and run toward a light in the window of the hut, faster than you could sprint in high school.

In the darkness, you misjudge where the door is. You run into it hard and fall to your knees. You get up and feel for the handle. You press down on the latch, pull the door open, jump inside and swing the door shut behind you.

Your palms are pressed against the door, your arms outstretched. Your heart feels like it's going to explode. Your head droops. Your whole body is shaking.

One of your friends steps into the kitchen, where you're standing. He asks what's going on.

You tell him you saw a grizzly, up close.

You're full of crap, he says.

You go into the main room of the hut. You tell all your friends what happened.

You're known for your practical jokes. Not a single friend says he believes you.

But that night, no one else ventures out to pee.

Scouts

Sipping his water, he tried to remember anything from her profile that he could ask her about. Oddly, the only thing he could recall was that she was in the Scouts.

"So I see you were in the Scouts," he said.

"Yes."

"Single sex or combined?"

"Single sex."

"Do you mind sharing why?"

"Not at all. I was in the Girl Scouts. But when they started letting boys in, I quit."

"That's funny. I quit the Boy Scouts when they started letting girls in."

Until then, she hadn't noticed his strong jawline, and he hadn't noticed the soft curve of her cheek.

Change of Heart

Walter hated working second shift, but jobs were scarce, and he had a young family to support. *I should be grateful*, he thought.

Still, tonight, as he began walking the 19 blocks to the row house he rented, Walter felt resentful that he couldn't afford a car.

A light snow began falling just as he was walking by a shanty-town, where women and children huddled together under cardboard roofs and men searched for anything they could burn.

When he got home, Walter felt grateful that he could kiss his wife and children good night as they slept in their beds.

Small Differences

I stepped up and knocked on the front door. I never knock. I always ring the bell, but I knew she hated that doorbell. She used to wince when she heard it. She thought it sounded tinny. *Maybe she's replaced it by now*, I thought. I didn't want to take a chance, though. So I knocked.

I heard footsteps. I could tell they were hers. It's funny, but if you live with someone long enough, you get to know even the sound of their footsteps. Hers were light and quick, like the patter of gentle rain. Mine are heavy and slow, more like thunder. She was always in a hurry. I like to take my time.

It made me think back to when we were newly married and just getting used to living together. How different we were. I was a meat-and-potatoes guy. She liked pasta. I took showers. She took baths. I drank coffee. She drank tea.

These were little things, of no consequence really, except they used to make me stop and realize I was now living with someone quite different from me, and discovering our differences was exciting. It kept me guessing. It made me look forward to being with her so that I could experience the unfolding of yet another mystery, however small.

Thirty years later, all those mysteries had vanished, and our differences now divided us. What had once been appealing, even alluring, had become a source of irritation.

We left each other to be happy again. At first, I was happier.

Everything was easier. But then my life became bland. I realized I missed the sound of bathwater running and her singing in the bathtub. I missed the sweet aroma of tea and how she always sipped it as she graded papers.

Her footsteps, though still faint, were coming closer. I heard the lock click open, as I had ten thousand times before. I didn't know if this was going to work, but I was glad I hadn't rung the bell.

Shiny Objects

"Let me see your spoons," Alex would say to his friends in the school cafeteria.

He would take their spoons, place the stems between the fingers of his right hand and bounce them between the palm of his left hand and his knee. After he played a while, he would slip the spoons into his pockets. Nobody ever missed them.

Alex did this well into his adult years. He played the spoons in restaurants and at parties. Everyone was so impressed that they forgot to ask for their spoons back.

At 40, Alex retired and moved to the Caribbean, having sold the last of his spoons for scrap.

Hello

She waited on the landing, her hands gripping the metal railing. Her face burned with anticipation. Her pulse beat hard in her ears.

Why hadn't she asked for his photo?

She scanned the men's faces. Too young. Too old.

Then she saw him stepping up the escalator. She knew his face instantly.

She had given him up 30 years before. She had known it was the right thing to do. But at what price? For 30 years, she'd longed to hold him, to look into his eyes, to know he was safe. But now that she saw him, she froze. After 30 years of longing to speak with him, she didn't know what to say.

He sensed her unease.

"Hello," he said, embracing her.

"Hello," she said, holding him close.

Sparkle

He pulled open the door of the bar and peeked inside. The afternoon sunlight through the doorway made the bottles behind the bar sparkle like rock candy.

It made him think of the penny candy in a long row of square glass jars just inside the front door of Seeger's, the corner store in the neighborhood where they grew up.

They had been childhood sweethearts. They would walk to Seeger's, holding hands, on Saturday mornings. He happily covered the cost of her root beer barrels and lemon drops with his allowance.

Years later, he handed over his last dollar to buy her wedding ring. She wore it for more than 60 years. She loved to watch the diamond sparkle in the sunlight.

Now, as rays of sunlight danced across the colored bottles behind the bar, he knew he would give everything he had ever owned to see the sparkle in her eyes once again.

The Kiss

They were both 12, neither children nor adults. Their families were close and, growing up, being together had always been so easy.

But lately they had become careful around each other. She worried about how she looked. He worried about what he said.

Today, though, as they walked a familiar country path, and the July sun warmed their bodies and birds sang and bees buzzed and their hands touched as they strayed from the hard dirt into the soft grass, they stopped walking and faced each other and closed their eyes.

Their lips met, and the world and all its cares fell away.

About the Author

After a long career in the corporate world, Don Tassone has returned to his creative writing roots, living the passion for the written word which first led him to earn his degree in English.

Small Bites is his third work of fiction, his second collection of short stories. His novel, *Drive*, and short story collection, *Get Back*, both appeared in 2017.

Besides writing, Don teaches Public Relations courses at Xavier University in Cincinnati. He and his wife Liz live in Loveland, Ohio. They have four children.

CPSIA information can be obtained
at www.ICGtesting.com
Printed in the USA
FFOW02n1625050518
46425298-48259FF

9 781936 135554